Wrong Window!

by Billy Van Zandt
& Jane Milmore

A SAMUEL FRENCH ACTING EDITION

SAMUEL FRENCH

FOUNDED 1830

NEW YORK HOLLYWOOD LONDON TORONTO

SAMUELFRENCH.COM

ISBN 978-0-573-69832-3   Printed in U.S.A.   #29621

MUSIC USE NOTE

Licensees are solely responsible for obtaining formal written permission from copyright owners to use copyrighted music in the performance of this play and are strongly cautioned to do so. If no such permission is obtained by the licensee, then the licensee must use only original music that the licensee owns and controls. Licensees are solely responsible and liable for all music clearances and shall indemnify the copyright owners of the play and their licensing agent, Samuel French, Inc., against any costs, expenses, losses and liabilities arising from the use of music by licensees.

IMPORTANT BILLING AND CREDIT
REQUIREMENTS

All producers of *WRONG WINDOW!* *must* give credit to the Author of the Play in all programs distributed in connection with performances of the Play, and in all instances in which the title of the Play appears for the purposes of advertising, publicizing or otherwise exploiting the Play and/or a production. The name of the Author *must* appear on a separate line on which no other name appears, immediately following the title and *must* appear in size of type not less than fifty percent of the size of the title type.

WRONG WINDOW! opened May 23, 2008, at the Brookdale College Performing Arts Center, in Lincroft, New Jersey, under the direction of Mark Fleming. It was produced by Noel Kubel and Jack Ryan. The assistant director was Francesca Vannucci, with set design by Noel Kubel, light and sound design by Chris Woolley, costume design by Kitty Cleary, and properties by Jen Lucero. Photography was by Danny Sanchez, graphic design was by Kevin Cosme, and the stage manager was Lauren Cervasio. The cast was as follows:

MARNIE ELBIES . . . . Jane Milmore

JEFF ELBIES . . . . Billy Van Zandt

ROBBIE . . . . Glenn Jones

MIDGE . . . . Susan Travers

THOR LARSWALD . . . . .Art Neill

LILA LARSWALD . . . . .Jennifer Bukavec

LOOMIS . . . . Jeff Babey

DETECTIVE DOYLE THOMAS . . . . .Geoff Shields

and the birds played themselves...

CHARACTERS

Marnie Elbies

Jeff Elbies

Robbie

Midge

Thor Larswald

Lila Larswald

Loomis

Detective Doyle Thomas

ACT ONE

Scene One

(Curtain rises on a New York high-rise apartment, taste-fully furnished. An older building. An upstage left door leads to the apartment building hallway. A downstage left archway leads off to the kitchen area. An upstage right door opens to a coat closet. A downstage right arch-way leads off to the bedroom/bathroom area.)

(A large picture window takes the entire upstage wall, out of which we can see across a courtyard into a mirror apartment.)

*(AT RISE, it is dusk. **MARNIE ELBIES** is staring out the upstage window through a large pair of binoculars. She is dressed for a night on the town. **JEFF ELBIES** enters from the stage left archway to see her spying at window.)*

JEFF. Through her rear window and the eye of her power-ful binoculars she was spellbound watching a great city tell on itself, exposing its cheating ways...

MARNIE. *(still looking out window)* Don't make fun of my hobbies. I have to tell you, not much has changed in the year I've been gone, Jeff. The bald guy in 6C still plays the piano with no pants on.

JEFF. Shame on you, spying on our neighbors. How would you feel if...

(taking out binoculars to spy on something across the way)

Whoa, Nellie.

MARNIE. Who is that?

JEFF. Nellie. In ten C. She moved in last month.

MARNIE. Wow. Those are not real.

JEFF. Of course they're real – they just knocked a lamp off the table.

(MARNIE laughs, looks at JEFF.)

MARNIE. Oh, my. Don't you look handsome.

JEFF. Yes, yes I do.

(She looks him over with her binoculars.)

MARNIE. Best view in the building.

JEFF. Be careful with those things. Objects may appear larger than they actually are, so don't get too excited.

(MARNIE puts down the binoculars and straightens JEFF's tie.)

MARNIE. Too late.

(MARNIE puts her arms around him and they kiss.)

JEFF. I'm so happy you moved back home.

MARNIE. Me, too. Let's not do that ever, ever again.

JEFF. I believe it was you, Mrs. Elbies, who wanted some time apart. I was perfectly happy with us and our "predictable" marriage. But then again, I am an unexciting stick-in-the-mud.

MARNIE. I said that?

JEFF. I'm afraid you did.

MARNIE. Can we just blame it on a mid-life crisis?

JEFF. If you like. You know, I was thinking of having one myself. Can you see me? I could dye my hair blonde, buy a Porsche, and walk around the apartment in a Speedo.

MARNIE. *(giggling as she kisses his neck)* Please don't.

(They kiss.)

(SFX: BUZZER)

(It is loud and jarring.)

That's Robbie and Midge.

JEFF. Do they always sound like that? Remember where we left off.

(JEFF *opens the door.* ROBBIE *and* MIDGE *enter. They are best friends and neighbors from the building. They are dressed for dinner.* ROBBIE *carries a bottle of champagne.*)

ROBBIE. Hey, what's the big idea? You look nicer than we do.

MIDGE. That's because they're madly in love.

ROBBIE. So are we.

MIDGE. We are? Oh, that's right.

JEFF. Champagne. Is that for us?

ROBBIE. Unless you have a boat for us to christen.

JEFF. I'll get some glasses.

(JEFF *exits to the kitchen.* ROBBIE *starts to follow.*)

ROBBIE. Glad you're back, Marnie.

MARNIE. Me, too.

ROBBIE. We missed you.

(ROBBIE *exits to the kitchen.*)

MIDGE. *(sotto)* You sure about this – getting back together?

MARNIE. Yes!

MIDGE. He still hardly ever leaves the building during the day.

MARNIE. He's going to therapy for that.

MIDGE. I know. It's just that he doesn't seem any different. If I were you I would have gone with that young editor who worked on your last book. What was his name, Ian?

MARNIE. Yes. He's too young. And I love Jeff.

MIDGE. You'd have to – to move back into New York City in July.

(JEFF *and* ROBBIE *return with four glasses.*)

JEFF. Here you go, Midge. Come and get your Irish on.

ROBBIE. How was California?

MARNIE. Beautiful. Sunny. Lonely.

JEFF. A toast –

(Brownout)

(The lights flicker and go out, along with the air conditioner which whines down.)

(SFX: AC WINDS DOWN)

(Then the power pops back on.)

(SFX: AC BLOWER STARTS UP [fade out as scene continues])

JEFF. What the – Dammit.

MIDGE. Another brownout. Third one this week!

ROBBIE. Please don't let the AC go out. At least you didn't have brownouts in California.

MARNIE. Actually, we did.

ROBBIE. You did? Man, they steal everything from us out there. They stole the Dodgers. The movie business. Police brutality.

MIDGE. They can't steal our seasons.

MARNIE. Oh, they have their own seasons. Earthquake, fire, mudslide, and TV pilot.

*(All laugh. **JEFF** toasts.)*

JEFF. A toast – to great friends. And to coming home.

MAN'S VOICE. *(off)* Go screw yourself.

(They look around, confused.)

JEFF. Excuse me?

ROBBIE. Where'd that come from?

FEMALE VOICE. *(off)* Maybe I will! It'll be a lot better than waiting around for you to do something!

*(They stop and try to place the direction of the noise. In the apartment across the courtyard. We see **THOR LAR-SWALD** [50's], a huge threatening-looking man in a wife beater t-shirt and work pants. He argues with **LILA LAR-SWALD**, his sexy younger wife who wears a body hugging yoga leotard.)*

MARNIE. That's the Larswalds. And I don't think they're talking to us.

JEFF. I hope not.

MIDGE. That's pretty loud.

MARNIE. It's the courtyard. You know how it acts like a megaphone.

MIDGE. Hear anything juicy?

MARNIE. Not really. I try not to eavesdrop.

JEFF. She's such a liar.

(A bird appears unnoticed on the ledge outside the Elbie's window. The argument continues in the upstage apartment. Most of the following words are muffled.)

LILA. *(off)* I don't know where you're getting these stories from. Nothing happened!

THOR. *(off)* My ass, nothing happened! You know how this makes me look?

(Another bird appears on the ledge unnoticed.)

MARNIE. I can't hear everything they're saying.

MIDGE. I know. They're too far away.

ROBBIE. Move closer to the window.

(They all move in to hear better. JEFF *sees the birds and flips out.)*

JEFF. Birds!!

(The others react as the bird flies away. JEFF *is frozen solid, sweating and panicked.)*

(The light continues to grow darker throughout the scene.)

MARNIE. Omigod. Jeff. Jeff?

*(*JEFF *can't breathe.)*

MIDGE. It's okay, Jeff. It's gone.

ROBBIE. Look at him. He's sweating like he has malaria.

MARNIE. Honey? Jeff? Are you okay?

JEFF. Can't…breathe.

MARNIE. Breathe slow. It's okay.

MIDGE. I thought he was seeing somebody about that.

ROBBIE. He is. But it doesn't mean that the guy's any good.

MARNIE. Jeff. Jeff? He's coming around.

JEFF. I'm okay. I'm okay. I'm sorry. Sorry. I have to sit.

MARNIE. You poor thing.

(They help him to the sofa. He still can't breathe.)

MIDGE. It's gotta be tough living in the City when you're afraid of birds. There are more birds per square inch here than anywhere on Earth – except the arm of that old lady in "Mary Poppins."

MARNIE. His therapist says he's doing better. Really.

JEFF. *(lightening the mood)* Yeah, I can eat Bird's Eye frozen peas now.

MIDGE. I can't imagine what it's like living with that.

*(**MIDGE** shoots **MARNIE** a look that gives double meaning to her words.)*

MARNIE. Everybody's afraid of something.

MIDGE. Yeah. Normal things. Vertigo. Ventriloquist dummies. People with small hands. But nothing like that.

ROBBIE. Midge, if you were on vacation in Bodega Bay and a seagull flew inside your car causing a ten car accident and you wound up in a body cast for six months, I think you'd be afraid of birds, too.

*(**MARNIE** gets his champagne. Behind them, the shades are lowered in the Larswald apartment.)*

MARNIE. Here. Drink this. There are no birds in here. That was five years ago and you are so much better now.

*(**MARNIE** hands him his glass.)*

JEFF. Thank you. I'm sorry.

THOR. Shut up!

ROBBIE. There he goes again. Shut up yourself. Hey, they lowered the shades.

MARNIE. That guy creeps me out.

MIDGE. He's a psycho. And he's been acting even weirder since you moved back.

MARNIE. I noticed that, too. Why do you suppose that is?

ROBBIE. Maybe 'cause you stare at him with binoculars while he beats his wife.

JEFF. I think it's just that they wanted our apartment and were hoping we'd get a divorce and move out.

MIDGE. Why? They have the same apartment you do.

MARNIE. Yes, but we have the renovated kitchen and bath.

(They hear more of a fight. We can only make out every other word.)

THOR. I should have expected this. You were a whore when I met you and you're always gonna be a whore. Why don't you just get the hell out!

LILA. Who's gonna make me, big man? You? You're all talk! Nothing but talk!

THOR. Yeah? Here's some talk!

(A horrible thud.)

MARNIE. What was that?

(The argument continues in the Larswald apartment. Their dialogue is MUFFLED. The foursome plasters itself against walls to eavesdrop better.)

MARNIE. What's he saying?

ROBBIE. Can't make it out.

MARNIE. Open the front door. Maybe we can hear down the hallway.

(JEFF opens the front door. We hear more muffled arguing.)

MARNIE. Can you hear them?

JEFF. Not really. He either said 'I'm going to kill you' or 'can you get me a glass of water.'

MIDGE. Something's going on over there, that's for sure. I wonder if it's about another man.

(JEFF spills his champagne.)

MARNIE. Jeff! Are you all right?

JEFF. Fine. I'm fine. Sorry. Thought it was a bird.

MARNIE. Why do you think there's another man?

MIDGE. Oh, you know. Rumors around the laundry room.

JEFF. Rumors? You can't listen to rumors. God, I'd hate to hear what people say about Marnie and me.

MIDGE. Yes, you would.

ROBBIE. Hey, are we going to eat or what?

MARNIE. Okay. Let me get my earrings. I'll be right back.

MIDGE. I'm coming with you. I want to see the new furniture.

(to boys)

Keep an ear out.

*(**ROBBIE** makes his ears stick out with his fingers. **MIDGE** laughs. **MARNIE** exits to the bedroom. **MIDGE** goes with her.)*

ROBBIE. Good, she's gone. Where's the new girl Nellie with the big fake bazookas?

*(**ROBBIE** grabs the binoculars. **JEFF** grabs them back and sets them down, anxious to discuss something before the girls get back.)*

JEFF. Robbie. I have something to tell you. But you've got to swear not to tell anybody.

ROBBIE. Are you gay?

JEFF. What? No! Why would you say that?

ROBBIE. Sorry, I had a conversation with my brother that started the exact same way. Sorry. What did you want to tell me?

*(**JEFF** looks off to the bedroom and back.)*

JEFF. All right. Here it is. Marnie can never know about this. But while she and I were separated and she was in L.A...I had an affair with Lila.

ROBBIE. Whoa.

JEFF. I know. It was very short-lived, and stupid. It should never have happened. But it did. I've been sick about it ever since. I can't let Marnie know. She'd never for-give me. Promise me you won't say anything.

ROBBIE. I promise. I just have one question.

JEFF. What's that?

ROBBIE. Who's Lila?

JEFF. Lila Larswald. The woman we just heard fighting with her husband.

ROBBIE. The sexy yoga teacher? Wow. You *really* aren't gay.

JEFF. Shh!

ROBBIE. Who could blame you?

JEFF. Marnie. I think Marnie could blame me pretty good.

ROBBIE. Wow, you downward dog, you. Why didn't you ever tell me?

JEFF. She's married. I felt like a creep and I ended it. If I told you, you might tell Midge, and she might tell Marnie and…What's the difference? The point is, I think that's what they're fighting about over there.

ROBBIE. Man, she's hot.

(*The girls return. There's a slight beat, and then* **ROBBIE** *continues.*)

As I was saying…the only thing we see from our apart-ment is Mr. MacGuffin in 4D. He's always sitting on his toilet with the door open facing our dining room table. And sometimes he waves at me. I think there's something wrong with him.

JEFF. You think?

MIDGE. We eat out a lot now.

MARNIE. Jeff, have you seen my topaz earrings? I can't find them anywhere.

JEFF. Really? That's the second pair you've lost since you moved back. I'll buy you new ones. A new start. New earrings.

MIDGE. That's so romantic. When's the last time you bought me earrings, Robbie?

ROBBIE. You don't need them. Your ear lobes are long enough as it is. Besides, you get any more jewelry and our side of the building is going to tilt.

THOR. You think this is funny?

LILA. Yes, I do. You're the biggest joke I know!

MARNIE. There they go again.

(*More muffled fighting between the upstage couple. Only a few words can be made out. But the tone is crystal clear. Ugly and abusive.*)

THOR. Wipe that smile off your face!

FEMALE VOICE. (*off*) Shut up, up there!

THOR. Shut up yourself, down there, you sour bitch!

LILA. Happy? The whole building can hear you!

THOR. Let 'em! I'm through with you! I'll send you back to Dublin in a boat with your beer smellin' mother! See how you like that?

LILA. Leave me alone! Don't you touch me, you fat pig!

(*The girls are mesmerized. At the same time they feel guilty and giggle.*)

JEFF. So, are we going to go eat?

ALL. Shhh!

MARNIE. In a minute. I want to hear what happens.

JEFF. Marnie. Mind your own business.

MARNIE. Leave me alone. You can't go out until it's dark out anyway.

ROBBIE. No birds out at night.

MIDGE. What about owls?

(**JEFF** *reacts.*)

ROBBIE. What are they fighting about?

MARNIE. Can't tell. But I bet it's about sex.

ROBBIE. It's definitely about sex.

MIDGE. You can't even hear them. How do you know it's about sex?

ROBBIE. I pretty sure I heard the words "up yours."

(SFX: A VASE SMASHES in the Larswald apartment.)

JEFF. Jeez. What was that?

(They stare and see nothing.)

MARNIE. Should we call someone?

JEFF. No. It's none of our business. Stop looking over there.

MIDGE. I love this. It's like a free show before we go to dinner.

(It is now completely dark out.)

(More muffled fighting. Suddenly we see the silhouette of a man lifting a woman's body and carrying her off.)

MARNIE. Omigod. What's he doing now?

MIDGE. Is she naked? She looks naked! Isn't that the silhouette of a naked woman?

ROBBIE. It certainly is. Jackpot!

(silence)

MARNIE. Ooh! Headed for the bedroom.

JEFF. Show's over, I guess.

MIDGE. What a gyp. Right when it gets to the good part.

ROBBIE. Looks like it's time for a little tantrum sex.

MARNIE. You mean tantric sex.

ROBBIE. Not the way they're doing it.

(They all laugh.)

(to JEFF, concerned, sotto) You okay?

(The girls look befuddled.)

JEFF. Of course I'm okay. Why wouldn't I be okay? You okay?

ROBBIE. Yeah.

JEFF. Okay then.

MIDGE. Damn. You can't see in the bedroom from here.

MARNIE. Not from the bathroom either – even if you stand on the tub.

(off their looks)

MARNIE. *(cont.)* Not that I ever tried to do that.

*(**MIDGE** studies other neighbors apartments.)*

MIDGE. Well, then who else have you got?

(All look off in a different direction.)

ROBBIE. Third floor down, the one with the torn curtain.

LADY. *(off)* Hey! What are you looking at?!

*(Laughing, the foursome plasters itself against the sides of the window walls so as to not be seen. Once they are out of sight, **THOR LARSWALD** stares out from behind his shade into their apartment. Seeing nothing he lowers his shade again. The foursome pops back out and sneaks one last look at the lady who yelled.)*

(off) Take a good look, you perverts!

(All react.)

ROBBIE. My eyes!

JEFF. Oh, that was ugly.

MIDGE. I can never look her in the face again.

MARNIE. That wasn't her face.

JEFF. Dinner?

MARNIE. God, yes.

(The girls grab their purses, and the foursome heads out the front door stage left)

ROBBIE. *(rubbing his eyes)* I think I'm gay now.

MIDGE. Yeah, blame her.

*(The **FOURSOME** exits. The silhouette of **THOR**, looking remarkably like Alfred Hitchcock, goes by the upstage window and poses at center.)*

(blackout)

Scene Two

(JEFF & MARNIE'S APARTMENT – TWO DAYS LATER – AFTERNOON)

(JEFF enters from the front door returning from a trip to the downstairs mailbox. He goes through a bundle of mail. He finds a manila envelope. Curious, he opens it. He thumbs through some naked Polaroids.)

JEFF. What the hell…?

(He checks the envelope for a return address. He looks inside the envelope. He reacts. Looks to the apartment behind him, and back to the Polaroids. MARNIE enters the apartment all excited and carrying flyers. He hides the photos in the envelope.)

MARNIE. Jeff! Jeff! Omigod. You are not going to believe this. It's all over the news. She's missing. She's missing!

JEFF. Who's missing?

MARNIE. Lila Larswald. Who do you think?

JEFF. What?

(MARNIE hands him a flyer.)

MARNIE. Look at this. There are flyers up and down the street. I told you something happened the other night.

JEFF. Lila's missing?

MARNIE. What are we going to do about it?

JEFF. What do you mean? What are we going to do about what?

MARNIE. Well, we can't just sit here.

JEFF. We're standing.

MARNIE. Jeff.

JEFF. Sorry. What exactly do you expect us to do?

MARNIE. We should call the police.

JEFF. And tell them what? We don't know where she is.

MARNIE. That's because she's probably dead.

JEFF. Dead? What are you talking about? How did you jump to that?

MARNIE. It's an obvious conclusion. Thor Larswald killed her.

JEFF. Marnie, slow down. This isn't one of your books. Nobody killed anyone. We didn't witness anything.

MARNIE. Is she missing or what?

JEFF. Yes, but –

MARNIE. Coincidentally right after the big fight we saw.

JEFF. We saw them fight. But then we saw them go off to the bedroom to have sex.

MARNIE. No, we didn't. We saw him carry what looked like a lifeless body to the bedroom. And now she's missing. The police are going to want to know what we heard and saw.

(**MARNIE** *goes to the phone.* **JEFF** *stops her.*)

JEFF. All we saw were shadows. And all we heard was *(inaudible mumbling).*

MARNIE. Are you making fun of me?

JEFF. Well, yes, I think I am.

MARNIE. But –

JEFF. I'm sorry, but you sound like a lunatic. We're having an argument right now. But that doesn't mean I'm going to kill you.

(in evil voice)

Or does it?

MARNIE. Jeff, 99 percent of the time when a woman is missing, it's because she's dead. And it's usually the husband who killed her. Or the boyfriend.

(**JEFF** *reacts.*)

JEFF. That can't be true.

MARNIE. Yes, it is. I've sold nine best-selling gothic murder mysteries. I know how it works. Murder victims almost always know their murderers. I didn't imagine what happened the other night. The four of us might have been the last people to see Lila alive. Aren't you even concerned?

JEFF. Yes. About you over-reacting. You call the police now and they find out who you are and it'll look like some kind of bad taste publicity stunt. Maybe Lila and Thor had a fight and she went to her mother's. You ever think about that?

(SFX: BUZZER)

MARNIE. Then she'd be at her mother's. Not missing.

(The door opens, revealing **MIDGE** *who is carrying flyers, too.)*

MIDGE. Oh, my God. Did you guys see this – ?

MARNIE. Jeff won't let me call the police.

MIDGE. Neither will Robbie. He says we've called so many times about Mr. MacGuffin and his open bathroom door they'd just think I was a nutjob anyway.

JEFF. Is Robbie downstairs?

MIDGE. Yes. He's installing mirrors on our window to try and blind Mr. MacGuffin.

*(***JEFF*** takes the envelope off the desk.)*

JEFF. Good. I have to talk him about something. While I'm gone, feel free to let your imaginations run wild.

MARNIE. Sure. Make fun of my imagination. That's how I make a living.

JEFF. Yeah? Well, here's a good title for your next book: "Milady, Mind Your Own Business." And don't call anybody!

*(***JEFF*** exits. The girls look at the Larswald apartment and back to the flyers.)*

MARNIE. *(staring at the flyer)* Isn't it awful?

MIDGE. I've seen her look better.

MARNIE. I mean about her being missing.

MIDGE. I think something bad happened the other night.

MARNIE. So do I. I wish we could find some proof.

(They both look across at the apartment.)

MIDGE. Of what?

MARNIE. Where she is, where she went. If she's, you know, even alive.

MIDGE. You think she's dead?

MARNIE. Don't you?

MIDGE. Yes, but I didn't want to say it.

MARNIE. I wish we could get in there and look around.

MIDGE. In where?

MARNIE. Their apartment, what do you think? Thor's at work. I saw him leave this morning. I know his schedule. We're good for a few hours at least.

MIDGE. Oh, Marnie, I don't know.

MARNIE. I do.

MIDGE. How would we even get in?

MARNIE. Like this.

(**MARNIE** *goes to the phone and dials.*)

MIDGE. Who are you calling? Jeff said not to –

MARNIE. Loomis? This is Mrs. Elbies in 10B. Could you come up here, please? It's an emergency. Thanks.

(*She hangs up.*)

MARNIE. He'll be right here. He's painting the empty apartment down the hall.

MIDGE. Loomis isn't going to let you in their apartment.

MARNIE. I know that. I'm going to slip their apartment key off his key ring. He uses his passkey anyway. He'll never know it's missing.

MIDGE. Won't he notice you grabbing at his pants?

MARNIE. Not if you're distracting him. All you have to do is flirt with him.

MIDGE. With Loomis?

MARNIE. Yes. You still remember how to flirt, don't you?

MIDGE. Yes. It's been a few years. But, yeah, I think I can catch a handyman's eye if I have to.

(*SFX: BUZZER*)

LOOMIS. Mrs. Elbies? It's Loomis.

(MARNIE lets in LOOMIS, a crusty, semi-retarded handy-man. He is paint spattered.)

MARNIE. Hello, Loomis. Thank you for coming up right away.

LOOMIS. No problem. So what's the problem? Forgive the pun.

MIDGE. What pun?

MARNIE. Oh. Uh…I was wondering if you could take a look at my closet doorknob. You know, the one you've been promising to fix since before I moved away.

LOOMIS. That's your emergency?

(makes game show buzzer sound)

No can do. I don't carry all my tools with me at one time. You know how many wrenches I have? How many paint brushes? How many screwdrivers?

(He waits for an answer.)

MARNIE. I'm supposed to answer that? No idea.

LOOMIS. *(makes game show buzzer sound)* Twenty-three. Thirty-four. And nine. Oh, look at the time. I'll have to come back another time. Forgive the pun.

(He starts to exit.)

MARNIE. Wait. While you're here, can you at least…check the radiator and make sure it's turned off? It's supposed to break a hundred today. I think it might still be on. Even with the air conditioning. Don't you feel how hot it is in here?

(MARNIE motions to MIDGE to get flirting.)

MIDGE. *(in her best breathy sexy voice)* So hot.

(LOOMIS looks at MIDGE quizzically, then continues talking to MARNIE.)

LOOMIS. I don't know. You know how many things I have on my to do list? Mr. MacGuffin hasn't been able to flush his toilet for two days.

MIDGE. Yes, I know.

MARNIE. Oh, please? You're already here.

MIDGE. Please? It's so hot.

*(**MIDGE** unbuttons a button on her blouse and fans herself with it. **LOOMIS** stops to watch her. **MARNIE** moves behind **LOOMIS**. **MIDGE** starts to make flirting faces.)*

LOOMIS. *(to **MARNIE**)* Well, only because I'm such a big fan and...

*(to **MIDGE**)*

What's the matter with you? Constipated?

MIDGE. No. It's just that I'm sooooo hot.

LOOMIS. You don't have to tell me how hot it is. It's like a log flume ride in my pants.

*(As **MIDGE** fans herself again, behind **LOOMIS**' back **MARNIE** gets the key ring off his belt.)*

MIDGE. Good job.

LOOMIS. What?

MIDGE. You always do a good job.

*(**MARNIE** rifles through the keys looking for the correct one.)*

MIDGE. Every single time I pass you on the stairs and see you hauling out a big bag of garbage or hosing down the dog crap on the sidewalks, I have to stop and watch you. I don't know what it is.

LOOMIS. *(makes game show buzzer sound)* I do. It's the uniform. Makes the ladies shakes in their panties. We all affect women like that. Firemen, handymen, crossing guards. Wearing this, I could have had old Mrs. Villars on the second floor if she hadn't, you know, had a heart attack and croaked the day the Pope came to New York.

MIDGE. Right. ...The radiator?

LOOMIS. I guess I could spare a few minutes.

(He hitches his belt.)

MIDGE. It's right over here.

(**MIDGE** *poses seductively against the wall near the radiator* **LOOMIS** *swaggers over. She pretends to melt.*)

MIDGE. Ooh, look at those big strong hands.

LOOMIS. Little lady, you ain't seen nothing yet.

(**LOOMIS** *bends over to feel the radiator, he exposes his butt crack.* **MARNIE** *and* **MIDGE** *react.* **LOOMIS** *feels all around the radiator.* **MARNIE** *moves behind* **LOOMIS**.)

That thing's as cold as old Mrs. Villars.

(*As* **LOOMIS** *bends over with* **MIDGE**, **MARNIE** *reaches past his plumber's crack and puts the ring back on* **LOOMIS**' *belt loop without his noticing.*)

(*She stands up and holds the key up behind his back to show* **MIDGE** *she's finished. But as she does, she accidentally drops the key down* **LOOMIS**' *plumber's crack.*)

(**MARNIE** *cringes at the idea of retrieving the key.* **MIDGE** *motions "just do it".* **MARNIE** *goes to reach down his crack but can't bring herself to do it. She builds up her courage, holds her nose and reaches for it, but suddenly* **LOOMIS** *stands up.* **MARNIE** *checks the floor for the key to fall out – it doesn't.*)

See? I told you. It's off.

(**MIDGE** *stares at* **MARNIE** *and shrugs.* **MARNIE** *slaps his back, then checks the floor – no key.*)

MARNIE. Hooray, it's off!

(**MARNIE** *takes* **LOOMIS** *by the hands and jumps up and down.*)

It's off! It's off!

(**MARNIE** *looks to the floor. No key. She does it again jumping harder.*)

It's off! It's off!

(**MIDGE** *joins in the jumping.*)

MIDGE. Hooray for Loomis!

LOOMIS. Easy. Easy. I just ate a taco. Ooh. Just threw up in my mouth a little bit.

(The key falls out of his pant leg and hits the floor.)

LOOMIS. What was that?

MARNIE. It's nothing. I dropped a quarter.

*(**MARNIE** quickly pockets the key and shoves him towards the door.)*

MARNIE. Well, you better get back to painting that apartment. I've got to get back to working on my new book.

LOOMIS. Hey. You know what you should write? A sequel to "Scent of a Pirate." Ever think about "Scent of a Handyman?"

MARNIE. I'm thinking of it right now.

(BLACKOUT)

Scene Three

(THE LARSWALD APARTMENT – later)

(This is a mirror image of Jeff and Marnie's place, but decorated in stark modern furnishings. The door upstage right leads to the apartment building hallway. The downstage right archway leads off to kitchen. The door upstage left is a closet. And the archway downstage left leads off to the bedroom and bath. At rise the apartment is empty.)

*(Key rattles in the door. The door opens. **MARNIE** and **MIDGE** sneak inside on tiptoes. They look around.)*

MARNIE. You look over there. I'll look over here.

MIDGE. What are we looking for?

MARNIE. Clues.

MIDGE. Here's a clue. They have terrible taste.

MARNIE. Smells like death.

MIDGE. That's me. Sorry. I'm a little nervous.

MARNIE. I'll check the bathroom. If he killed her, he probably did it in there and washed her blood down the bathtub drain.

MIDGE. Eww.

*(**MARNIE** exits to the bedroom archway. Silence as **MIDGE** tiptoes around. **MIDGE** goes to open the closet door.)*

MARNIE. *(off)* No! Oh, no!!!

*(**MARNIE** enters from the bedroom with a dress.)*

MARNIE. Look at this. I bought the same dress at Sak's. And she got it for $200 less!

MIDGE. What else did you find?

MARNIE. Lila's clothes are all over the room. Her good jewelry is still in her jewelry box. And her make-up kit is sitting on the sink. That proves she's not on a trip. She's just gone.

MIDGE. What now?

MARNIE. The kitchen. I want to see the knives.

MIDGE. Put the dress back first.

MARNIE. *(handing* MIDGE *the porn)* Here. You do it. I want to check the –

*(*JEFF *and* ROBBIE *are seen at the upstage apartment window – staring, horrified that their wives are in the neighbor's apartment.)*

Look at those creeps in that apartment peeking at us.

MIDGE. That's your apartment.

MARNIE. Oh, my God, it is. It looks so different from here. That's Jeff and Robbie. Why are they waving at us?

MIDGE. They're not waving. They're trying to tell us something.

MARNIE. What?

(SFX: NOISE AT DOOR.)

MARNIE. Oh my God.

MIDGE. Shit.

MARNIE. Hide!

*(*MARNIE *and* MIDGE *panic and scramble.* MARNIE *hides in the kitchen.* MIDGE *hides in the bedroom taking the porn magazines with her.)*

*(*THOR LARSWALD *enters with a brown paper bag. He kicks off his shoes and starts taking off his shirt, revealing a wife-beater T-shirt, as he crosses for the bedroom.* MARNIE*'s head pops out of the kitchen archway, then ducks back.* THOR *exits to the bedroom. Silence.* MARNIE *sneaks out a few feet waiting for the worst.)*

(SFX: SHOWER)

*(*THOR *re-enters, still dressed, carrying a towel.* MARNIE *hides behind the sofa just in time.* THOR *tosses the towel on the sofa as he crosses to the kitchen with the paper bag.* MARNIE *pops up from behind the sofa.* MIDGE *enters from the bedroom, soaking wet – obviously she'd hidden in the shower.* MARNIE *grabs the towel and*

throws it on **MIDGE**'s *head.* **THOR** *starts to re-enter from the kitchen.* **MARNIE** *quickly pulls* **MIDGE** *and the towel into the closet.*)

(**THOR** *walks towards the bedroom archway. He slips on the water and falls. He rises, looks at the water on the floor.*)

THOR. What the...

(**THOR** *looks for the towel, it's missing. He must have left it in the bathroom. He exits to the bathroom, wondering how the water out into the living room. After he exits, the shower goes off.*)

(SFX: SHOWER OFF)

(**MARNIE** *and* **MIDGE** *peek out to see if the coast is clear. It is. They exit the closet and race to the front door.*)

(SFX: BUZZER)

(*The girls panic and hide back in the closet.*)

(SFX: BUZZER)

(**THOR** *enters and goes to the front door.*)

Who is it?

JEFF. *(off)* Jeff Elbies.

(**THOR** *hesitates, then:*)

THOR. What do you want?

JEFF. Can you open the door? Please. It's very important.

(**THOR** *opens the door.* **JEFF** *tries peeking past* **THOR** *during the following. He holds a unopened newspaper rolled up in plastic.*)

THOR. What?

JEFF. Your newspaper's out here.

THOR. So? What do you want?

JEFF. What do you want?

THOR. What do you mean?

JEFF. What do YOU mean?

THOR. What's the matter with you? What are you doing here?

JEFF. *(trying to see past)* What are YOU doing here?

THOR. What do you mean, what am I doing here? I live here.

*(**MARNIE** and **MIDGE** peek out of the closet, see **THOR**'s back is to them.)*

JEFF. Did you get off work early?

*(**JEFF** steps right. **THOR** follows stepping to the right of the door frame.)*

THOR. I didn't go to work. My wife is missing.

*(**JEFF** signals the girls to exit behind **THOR**'s back.)*

JEFF. Oh, you know about that?

THOR. Yeah, I know about that. What do YOU know about that?

*(The **GIRLS** start tiptoeing to the door behind **THOR**'s back.)*

JEFF. Nothing. Why would I know anything about that?

THOR. You watch me. And now your wife is back and she watches me. You think I don't see you. But I see you.

*(**THOR** points behind him to their apartment. The girls quickly duck down behind the sofa. **THOR** steps back in front of the door frame, blocking the girls' exit.)*

If you know what's good for you, you'll mind your own business.

*(**JEFF** reacts.)*

Get the message?

JEFF. Yes. Yes, I did get your message. So what is it you want from me?

*(**THOR** goes to close the door.)*

THOR. I want you to get the hell out.

*(**JEFF** takes the newspaper back and drops it on the floor.)*

JEFF. Oh, sorry. Your paper.

(JEFF *pushes past him to pick up his paper and "accidentally" kicks it farther into the room. He continues to "accidentally" kick it farther away from the door each time he goes to pick it up.* THOR *follows in a few steps, turning his back to the door.*)

THOR. Get away from there. Stop kicking it.

(*The* GIRLS *sneak behind him and exit into the hallway.* ROBBIE *appears out of the hallway and holds the door for them. He ushers them out, and closes the door, staying in the room, motioning, "All Clear" to* JEFF *behind* THOR's *back.* THOR *starts to turn.*)

JEFF. No!

(ROBBIE *hits the floor and crawls behind the sofa, out of sight.*)

THOR. No what?

JEFF. No problem.

(JEFF *hands* THOR *the newspaper.* THOR *throws* JEFF *out the door. And the newspaper, too.*)

THOR. Get out of here.

(THOR *slams the door and locks it.* THOR *turns around in time to see* ROBBIE *stand up. A beat.*)

ROBBIE. *(incredulous)* What are you doing in my apartment?

THOR. This is my apartment.

(ROBBIE *looks around.*)

ROBBIE. My bad.

(ROBBIE *runs out.* THOR *locks the door behind him and scratches his head then slowly turns his head to stare into the Elbies apartment. He sees* JEFFREY, MARNIE *and* MIDGE *arguing intensely and pointing at* THOR's *apartment. They turn to see* THOR *looking back at them and immediately drop out of view. A beat later,* ROBBIE *enters their apartment and stands over them asking why they're ducked down. He looks over and sees* THOR *staring at him, and sinks from view, waving.* THOR *turns back, looks left, looks right and thinks to himself.*)

(*BLACKOUT*)

Scene Four

(JEFF & MARNIE'S APARTMENT – LATE THE NEXT MORNING)

(The apartment is empty. JEFF and MARNIE enter from the bedroom. JEFF is finishing dressing, MARNIE is still in a robe. MARNIE is playful.)

MARNIE. See? Sometimes fighting can be fun. You were so intense last night.

JEFF. Well, I was angry last night. But, you'll notice, I didn't kill you.

MARNIE. It was close.

JEFF. I still can't believe you went in there. You could have been arrested. Breaking and entering is still a crime the last time I checked. How did you get in there anyway?

(MARNIE crosses to the desk.)

MARNIE. *(embarrassed)* I stole Loomis' key.

(MARNIE holds it up.)

JEFF. What's the matter with you? Save some craziness for when the Altzheimer's kicks in.

(JEFF takes the key and puts it on the desk.)

What if you were right and something had happened over there? Did you really think pissing off the murderer was a good way to go?

MARNIE. No. But something has happened over there, Jeff. All her stuff is still there – she didn't take her clothes, her jewelry, her makeup. I just have a horrible feeling about all this. Something's not adding up. Thor's weird about me moving back in. Lila was, too. They have a fight. She disappears. Am I missing anything?

JEFF. No, that's all we know. That's about it. Nothing more to know.

(SFX: BUZZER)

Who is that?

(JEFF *looks off to* THOR*'s apartment.*)

MARNIE. I don't know. But answer it. I have to get dressed. It's Fourth of July and Midge and I are having lunch.

(MARNIE *goes off to the bedroom.* JEFF *crosses to the door, peeks through security hole. He opens the door and* ROBBIE *enters.*)

ROBBIE. Can I hide out in here?

JEFF. What happened?

ROBBIE. You know how I set up those mirrors to reflect light right into Mr. MacGuffin's eyes when he's doing his business?

JEFF. Yes.

ROBBIE. I think I set his hamper on fire. He's coming for me.

JEFF. Never mind that. Did you hide those pictures for me?

ROBBIE. Yes, I hid them in my special underwear drawer.

JEFF. What's your...never mind.

ROBBIE. You really think Thor sent those naked pictures of his wife to you?

JEFF. Who else? It was his way of telling me he knows about Lila and me.

(SFX: BUZZER)

ROBBIE. It's MacGuffin! Hide me. Hide me.

LOOMIS. (*off*) It's Loomis!

(MARNIE *enters from the bedroom, dressed for the day.*)

MARNIE. Hi, Robbie.

JEFF. Loomis? What's he doing here?

MARNIE. I asked him to fix the closet door.

JEFF. When?

MARNIE. A year ago.

JEFF. What's wrong with the closet door?

MARNIE. The handle's loose and it has a really weird squeak.

(**MARNIE** *opens the front door.* **LOOMIS** *enters.* **JEFF** *looks to the closet door.*)

LOOMIS. Sorry it took me so long. But the building is lousy with cops asking about Mrs. Larswald.

ROBBIE. Nothing about Mr. MacGuffin's hamper?

LOOMIS. What?

ROBBIE. Nothing.

JEFF. What are they asking?

LOOMIS. All kind of things, "who saw her last" "who she hung out with." Bottom line, she's still missing. It's a terrible thing. Terrible. Excuse the pun.

(looking out the window)

Boy, you can see right into their apartment from here. Have you seen anything suspicious?

JEFF. No. We've seen nothing. We have nothing to do with those people.

MARNIE. Well, actually we saw –

JEFF. Nothing. We've seen nothing. I can't see distances anyway. I have a stigmatism.

LOOMIS. Oh, yeah? My aunt had that. Saw Jesus Christ's face in a pancake. Weird broad.

JEFF. Well, anyway, no one's talked to us yet.

LOOMIS. Yeah. And you know why? 'Cause it's always the handyman! You want to catch a thief? It's the handyman. Your pain in the ass yapping dog disappears and they find it burned to a crisp in the incinerator? It's the handyman. Missing wife? It's the handyman! Cops started with me. And now they're going floor to floor – bottom up. They'll get to you guys soon enough.

JEFF. They will? What for? We don't know anything.

LOOMIS. *(makes game show buzzer sound)* I have the wrong tool box. This here's my electric fix-it box. Term we use in the trade. I need the small jobs and carpentry box. Another term. Sorry, Mrs. Elbies. I'll get it and be right back up.

JEFF. See you in another year.

(**MARNIE** *shoots another look.*)

MARNIE. I'll be out when you get back. But Mr. Elbies will be here. He saw a bird the other night. He won't be leaving the building for a few days.

LOOMIS. I'm a little afraid of birds, too. Ever since I saw that scary bird movie…what's it called? Oh, yeah. *March of the Penguins.*

(**LOOMIS** *exits.* **JEFF**, **MARNIE** *and* **ROBBIE** *share a look.*)

MARNIE. I have to go.

(*sotto*)

Thanks for the early Fourth of July fireworks.

(**MARNIE** *kisses* **JEFF** *goodbye.* **MARNIE** *and* **LOOMIS** *exit.*)

ROBBIE. What shall we do today? Want to rent *March of the Penguins?*

JEFF. I didn't know the closet was broken. What did she say, the handle's loose?

(**JEFF** *opens the door.*)

(*SFX: THEME TO "PSYCHO"-SOUNDING CLOSET DOOR SQUEAK*)

(**LILA LARSWALD**'s *dead body, falls forward and crumbles onto the floor.*)

(**JEFF** *and* **ROBBIE** *flip out.*)

JEFF/ROBBIE. Aaah!!! Omigod!!!!! Aaaahh!!!

(*Then they both freeze for a long pause. They look to each other in horror and shock. They look back to the body.*)

ROBBIE. Who is that?

JEFF. Lila. Lila Larswald.

ROBBIE. Boy, she sure looked different in those pictures. Jesus, is she dead?

JEFF. I don't know. Check her.

ROBBIE. You check her. You had the affair with her.

JEFF. Shut up!

(**JEFF** *feels her pulse.*)

I think she's dead.

ROBBIE. You think? What gave it away? The purple marks on her neck? Or the swollen tongue?

JEFF. Her nose is cold. Is that a good sign?

ROBBIE. For cocker spaniels. Not people.

JEFF. Shit.

ROBBIE. Oh, God. What do we do. Who do we call? 9-1-1 or Mary-Kate Olsen? Maybe I should just dial "M" for murder?

JEFF. Shut up. Let me think. Why the hell is her dead body in my closet?

ROBBIE. I don't know. Why IS her dead body in your closet?

(**ROBBIE** *backs away from* **JEFF.**)

JEFF. Oh, don't look at me like that. That son of a bitch Thor must have found out about us.

ROBBIE. You and me?

(**JEFF** *points wildly at* **LILA** *and himself.*)

JEFF. Me and her! That's why he sent those photos. He must have killed Lila in a jealous rage. Just like Marnie said.

ROBBIE. God, she's good.

JEFF. And now he's trying to frame me. What else could it be?

ROBBIE. I don't know. What else COULD it be?

(**ROBBIE** *backs away again.*)

JEFF. Oh, stop doing that. You don't seriously think I had anything to do with killing her, do you?

ROBBIE. No, no. I believe you. Whatever you say. Don't hurt me.

JEFF. You're an idiot. Oh, Jesus. What do we do. What do we do. What do we do. I know. We have to put the body back into her own apartment.

ROBBIE. I don't want to do that.

JEFF. We have to. How's it going to look if the girl I had an affair with is dead in my closet?

ROBBIE. Like you killed her?

(**ROBBIE** *backs away.*)

JEFF. Come on. We have to put her back in her own apartment.

ROBBIE. How?

JEFF. There's a key right here. And once we do, we can say we saw her dead body through the window and call the cops. Now, come on.

(*They look down at the body.*)

ROBBIE. How do we…?

JEFF. I don't know. Let's just lift her up.

ROBBIE. I never touched a dead body before.

JEFF. What, like I have!?

ROBBIE. I don't know. Have you?

JEFF. Knock it off. Come on. Pick her up.

ROBBIE. You pick her up. You're the one who didn't kill her.

JEFF. Wait a minute. We can't touch her. We'll leave fingerprints.

ROBBIE. You already touched her!

JEFF. Omigod, I did. Okay. I'll wipe her off.

(**JEFF** *opens the closet and takes out a bucket of cleaning supplies. He finds a pair of rubber gloves for himself and a pair for* **ROBBIE.**)

Here. Put these gloves on.

(*Business of putting on the rubber gloves.*)

They're too small. They don't even fit.

ROBBIE. Good. Then they must acquit.

(**JEFF** *pulls a bottle of cleaner and a rag and cleans his fingerprints off* **LILA**'s *wrist.*)

ROBBIE. Clean her off good, now.

JEFF. I am. Where else did I touch her?

*(**ROBBIE** takes the cleaner and sprays her breasts.)*

Since she's been dead!

ROBBIE. Oh. Uh, nowhere, then.

*(**JEFF** tosses the cleaning supplies back into the closet.)*

JEFF. Okay. Come on. Let's carry her.

ROBBIE. Do we have to?

JEFF. Yes. Let's do it together. Come on. It won't be so hard.

ROBBIE. Not yet, but wait a few hours.

JEFF. Okay. Let's go. You take one end I'll take the other.

(They both bend to lift her.)

Wait. We can't carry her down the hall. What if someone sees us? That would really put me under suspicion.
We'll be carrying a dead girl whose pictures are all over
this building.

ROBBIE. Well, it's not like she can carry us.

JEFF. Stop talking. Go in the bedroom and get the wig I
bought Marnie when I thought she had cancer.

*(**ROBBIE** dashes off to the bedroom.)*

I'm so sorry, Lila. Oh, God, I'm sorry.

*(**ROBBIE** returns with a blonde wig that looks like **MAR-
NIE**'s hair.)*

ROBBIE. Here.

JEFF. All right. Put it on her head.

*(**ROBBIE** starts for her, then stops short.)*

ROBBIE. I'm not touching her dead head.

JEFF. Stop being a baby and put the wig on her.

ROBBIE. You do it – you're such a big man.

JEFF. Fine. Give me that.

*(**JEFF** reluctantly puts the wig on **LILA**.)*

There. How's that?

ROBBIE. Nice. She looks good as a blonde.

JEFF. All right. Let's go. On three. One, two, three.

(JEFF *lifts* LILA's *body but* ROBBIE *does not.*)

I said on three.

ROBBIE. I always do one, two, three, lift.

JEFF. Fine. One, two, three, lift!

(ROBBIE *lifts.*)

I hadn't started yet.

ROBBIE. Oh.

JEFF. One, two, three, lift.

(*They lift the body. It starts to slip.* JEFF *catches it with one hand, twisting* LILA's *body as he does so. Her arms flail.*)

Okay. Let's go.

ROBBIE. Hey, can dead people sweat?

JEFF. I don't think so. Why?

ROBBIE. Ah, man. I don't want to know what that is.

(*As they get to the front door, at exactly the wrong moment...*)

(*SFX: BUZZER*)

LOOMIS. *(off)* It's Loomis.

JEFF. Shit.

(*calling off, stalling*)

Loomis who?

ROBBIE. Loomis the handyman.

JEFF. Shut up. I know it's Loomis the handyman.

(*The body starts to slide down. They grab it and stand it up.*)

LOOMIS. *(off)* Loomis the handyman.

JEFF. You answer the door. I'll put the body back in the closet.

*(**ROBBIE** agrees. **JEFF** lifts the body and heads past the sofa en route to the closet. Without waiting, **ROBBIE** immediately opens the door.)*

ROBBIE. Come on in.

JEFF. Not yet, I –

*(**JEFF**, thinking quickly, flips the body on to the sofa and then jumps on top of it to look like he's making out with it, draping **LILA**'s arms over his shoulders. **LOOMIS** enters with a different toolbox.)*

LOOMIS. I'm back.

ROBBIE. From what?

LOOMIS. I'm here to fix the closet. And...

*(**LOOMIS** sees **JEFF** and **MARNIE** making out on the couch. The corpse's arms slides off **JEFF**'s back. He picks it up and lays it on his back It slides off a second and third time. **JEFF** picks up her hand, licks it and "sticks it" to his back, then continues making out with **LILA**'s body.)*

I thought Mrs. Elbies went to lunch. What are they doing?

ROBBIE. Making out. Isn't that cute? Ever since they got back together they can't keep their hands off of each other.

*(**LOOMIS** looks at **ROBBIE**.)*

LOOMIS. What are you doing here?

ROBBIE. Just watching.

*(**LOOMIS** gives **ROBBIE** a strange look.)*

LOOMIS. I better fix that door.

*(**LOOMIS** opens the closet door.)*

(SFX: THEME TO "PSYCHO"-SOUNDING CLOSET DOOR SQUEAK.)

*(**LOOMIS** gasps.)*

ROBBIE. What? What's the matter? What do you see?

LOOMIS. I see I'm gonna need a new back plate.

> *(pointing to door knob)*
>
> Here's your problem. You care to see this, Mr. Elbies?
>
> **(JEFF** *waves him off and keeps making out.)*
>
> Jeez, I hope I have a strike plate that matches.
>
> **(ROBBIE** *closes the closet door.)*

ROBBIE. Get one from Mr. MacGuffin's bathroom door. He never uses his.

LOOMIS. I'll have to come back. Don't worry. I'll fix this for you in no time, Mrs. Elbies.

JEFF. *(falsetto)* Thank you. Please get out! Go away!

> **(LOOMIS** *goes to exit. He looks at* **ROBBIE.** *)*

LOOMIS. Aren't you leaving, too?

ROBBIE. Nah, I'm good.

> **(LOOMIS** *gives* **ROBBIE** *a look and exits, confused.* **JEFF** *rises up, disgusted and takes a fit.)*

JEFF. Argh!! Do you know what it's like to kiss a cold unresponsive woman with no control of her bodily fluids?

ROBBIE. Sadly, yes.

JEFF. Okay, look. You stay here in case Loomis comes back and I'll do this myself.

ROBBIE. And I'll stay here.

JEFF. Right. Get the door.

ROBBIE. And I'll get the door.

> **(JEFF** *throws* **LILA**'s *body over his shoulder and dashes out. The door closes.)*
>
> *(calling after)* Hey! How are you going to get in? You left the key on the desk… Jeff?
>
> **(ROBBIE** *runs to the desk. Business of him trying to pick up the key with rubber gloves on. He rushes to the front door with the key. When he opens it* **MARNIE** *is there. She startles him [and us].)*

MARNIE. Hi, Robbie.

ROBBIE. Ahh!

MARNIE. What are you still doing in here?

ROBBIE. What am I still doing in here?

MARNIE. I asked you first.

(**ROBBIE** *removes thew gloves behind* **MARNIE** *'s back.*)

ROBBIE. Jeff asked me to wait for Loomis. He's supposed to be fixing your closet.

MARNIE. And where's Jeff?

(*We see* **JEFF** *in the back apartment with* **LILA** *'s dead body over his shoulder. He crosses to* **THOR** *'s bedroom.*)

ROBBIE. Jeff who?

MARNIE. Jeff Goldblum. Who do you think I'm talking about?

ROBBIE. Oh, Jeff. He went somewhere to drop something off.

MARNIE. He went out?

ROBBIE. Not out-out. He's in the building. He's a…putting something in cold storage.

(**JEFF** *and* **LILA** *exit the window.*)

MARNIE. Oh. Can I ask you something?

ROBBIE. He didn't kill anyone. I can tell you that!

(**JEFF** *appears – alone – and exits the Larswald apartment.*)

MARNIE. What? No. I mean, is he okay? He doesn't seem any better now than he did before I left. He seems so…jumpy.

ROBBIE. Nah. He's doing MUCH better. And he's so happy you came back.

MARNIE. Really?

(**JEFF** *enters the apartment. The gloves and blonde wig hang out of his pocket – away from* **MARNIE** *'s view.* **JEFF** *shivers.*)

Hi, honey.

(**MARNIE** *goes to kiss him hello. He waves her off. He exits to bathroom making throat clearing gagging noises.*)

MARNIE. *(cont.)* See, what I mean?

(**MIDGE** *enters the open front door.*)

MIDGE. Marnie. Where the hell were you? You stood me up. I waited on that corner for an hour. And it's a hundred and two out there.

(SFX: **JEFF** *GARGLES.*)

MARNIE. Midge, I'm so sorry but you're not going to believe who I just saw...

(**JEFF** *enters, toothbrush in hand. He makes a few faces.* **ROBBIE** *sees the gloves and blonde wig hanging out of* **JEFF**'*s back pocket, grabs them and throws it off stage into the bedroom. The* **GIRLS** *don't see it.*)

Jeff, before you start yelling, just hear me out. I didn't plan it but when I left the building to meet Midge for lunch, who should be walking out of the lobby at exactly the same time as me but Thor Larswald?

MIDGE. No!

MARNIE. Yes! And, well, I couldn't help myself – I just started following him. Right out of the building and down into the subway.

MIDGE. No!

MARNIE. Yes. But he didn't see me. It was like we were strangers on a train. And then he got off and went to that French restaurant Les Halles on Park Avenue –

MIDGE. I love that place.

MARNIE. Me, too. You ever have the onion soup?

MIDGE. To die for.

MARNIE. So, anyway, I sit at the bar and you'll never guess what happens next.

ROBBIE. You order a drink?

MARNIE. No. I watched Thor meet this tall, beautiful, sexy woman. Wearing a leather skirt up to here. Obviously second wife material. He took her hand! And then they hugged each other, tight. Tight. It was really intense.

MIDGE. No!

MARNIE. Yes! I'm telling you – without a shadow of a doubt, he murdered his wife!

JEFF. I believe you. Let's call the police!

MARNIE. Really? What changed your mind?

JEFF. Let's just say I have a bad taste in my mouth.

(**JEFF** *clears his throat one last time, then crosses to the desk for his cell phone. He dials 9-1-1.*)

I'd like to report a murder. Mrs. Lila Larswald. No, I'm not Lila Larswald. That's who was murdered! 140 East 28th Street, apartment 10D. Yes. No, no no no no. We're all fine. But she's…dead. My name? Jeffrey Elbies. Yes. Okay. Thank you. Goodbye.

(**JEFF** *looks to* **ROBBIE** *and they both nod like they did the right thing. Suddenly in the rear apartment we see what appears to be* **LILA LARSWALD** *walk in front of the window in a pink terry bathrobe, fresh from the shower, toweling her hair dry.*)

MARNIE. Oh, my God. It's Lila!

JEFF/ROBBIE. She's alive????

(All react.)

(curtain)

ACT TWO

Scene One

(JEFF & MARNIE'S APARTMENT – LATER)

(It is dusk. Through out the following it get progressively darker outside. The Larswald apartment is lit up. We can see **THOR**, *a* **DETECTIVE** *and* **TWO POLICEMEN**. **MARNIE** *is standing by the window stage left deliberately not looking out the window,* **JEFF** *and* **ROBBIE** *are doing the same stage right.)*

MARNIE. What are they doing now?

*(**MIDGE** rises from behind the sofa with a cardboard periscope.)*

MIDGE. Can't tell. What a waste of money this was.

ROBBIE. I don't see "Lila" anywhere. Where'd she go?

MARNIE. She was drying her hair. She's probably getting dressed.

JEFF. How was "Lila" there in the first place?

MARNIE. Jeez, Jeff. You sound like you're sorry she's back.

JEFF. No, no. Nothing would make me happier than seeing Lila walk past that window.

MIDGE. Really.

ROBBIE. Yeah? Well, it would freak me out.

MIDGE. That guy in the suit must be in charge. He sure points a lot.

MARNIE. God, I need a drink. Martinis?

MIDGE. Sounds great.

MARNIE. Keep watching. We'll be right back.

*(The **GIRLS** exit to the kitchen.)*

ROBBIE. Boy, sure are a lot of cops over there.

JEFF. Maybe they found the body.

ROBBIE. The dead one?

JEFF. That's the only one there is. I don't get it. Who was that we saw walk past the window? There has to be a logical explanation.

ROBBIE. Hey…maybe it was his girlfriend.

JEFF. The girl he met today in the restaurant was blonde.

ROBBIE. How do we know that? We didn't see her.

JEFF. Marnie did. What, you think she's lying?

ROBBIE. I guess not. But none of this makes any sense to me.

JEFF. Well, I know for a fact that Lila's dead. I know I put her dead body in the tub. And I know it's impossible for a dead body to get up and walk past a window.

ROBBIE. Maybe it was Thor.

JEFF. He's a foot taller than she is and looks nothing like her.

ROBBIE. Not if he was on his knees. Look. If you're over there and looking over here. Would this look like Lila?

(**ROBBIE** *drops to his knees and walks past the window, acting girlie. The* COPS *stare at him and point.*)

JEFF. That looks nothing like Lila. You think I'd be attracted to that?

ROBBIE. Well, picture me with long brown hair. Now, how do I look?

(*He does it again, pretending his hair is flowing. The cops in the Larswald apartment think he's mocking them.*)

JEFF. Like a jack ass. It wasn't Thor.

(*The girls enter with martinis.*)

MARNIE. Anything?

(**MARNIE** *hands out the drinks.*)

ROBBIE. Nothing.

JEFF. What are they doing over there?

(*The* **DETECTIVE** *points towards the Elbies apartment.* **JEFF** *and* **ROBBIE** *hit the floor.* **THOR** *glares.* **MARNIE** *waves weakly. The detective and the police exit out* **THOR***'s apartment.*)

MARNIE. Oh, God. I think they're coming over here.

JEFF. Shit. Okay. Act nonchalant.

ROBBIE. I'm always nonchalant.

(*SFX: BUZZER*)

(**ROBBIE** *jumps.*)

JEFF. I'll get it.

(**JEFF** *turns on the wall sconces and answers the door.*)

(**DETECTIVE DOYLE THOMAS** *enters [40's]. He's a weathered plainclothes cop who's good at his job.*)

THOMAS. Mr. Elbies?

JEFF. Yes.

THOMAS. Detective Doyle Thomas. You're the one who called about your neighbor?

JEFF. Yes. Yes, I did.

THOMAS. May I come in?

JEFF. Of course. This is my wife, Marnie. And these are our neighbors, Mr. & Mrs. Smith – Robbie & Midge.

(*Ad lib hellos. The girls absent-mindedly toast him with their martinis.*)

THOMAS. (*ignoring the drinks for now*) You reported Mrs. Larswald was murdered?

(*No one speaks.*)

JEFF. Yessir.

THOMAS. Why did you do that, sir?

JEFF. "Why?"

THOMAS. Yes, why. What made you think the woman was dead?

ROBBIE. Smell his breath.

(JEFF *smacks* ROBBIE.)

JEFF. Oh. Well, we heard them fighting, and then she was missing, and we got to talking…and it just seemed like a logical conclusion. But two seconds after I called the police, we saw her drying her hair in the window.

MARNIE. We all did.

JEFF. So, you know, whoops.

MIDGE. We're just so glad she's okay.

JEFF. Sorry to have wasted your time, Officer.

THOMAS. We don't know that she IS okay. And I don't know what you think you saw. But Lila Larswald has not been seen since she was reported missing four days ago.

MARNIE. That's impossible. We all just saw her.

THOMAS. There is no sign that Mrs. Larswald has been in that apartment. Dead OR alive.

JEFF. Did you check the tub?

THOMAS. Yes!

MIDGE. But –

THOMAS. And I doubt she was taking a shower – it was bone dry.

ROBBIE. What do you mean, "bone" dry? Weren't there any fluids?

MARNIE. But we saw her.

THOMAS. *(eying the martinis)* Uh-huh. You know, it's a crime to call 9-1-1 with a false report.

MARNIE. Detective Thomas, maybe it wasn't a false report. When a person is missing – especially a woman – ninety percent of the time she's been murdered and most of the time it's by somebody she knows.

DETECTIVE THOMAS. *(sarcastic)* Is that right?

JEFF. Yeah. Somebody like her husband, for instance.

MARNIE. Or a boyfriend.

JEFF. But mostly the husband.

(All look at JEFF.)

JEFF. I mean, look at that guy.

ROBBIE. Yeah, he's got homicidal maniac written all over his face.

THOMAS. HE does, huh?

JEFF. His wife's missing. The lady vanishes and he's not even upset. He got real angry when we asked about her.

ROBBIE. Ballistic.

JEFF. Then today my wife sees him with another woman in a restaurant and they're hugging and holding hands.

THOMAS. When was this?

MARNIE. This afternoon. You know Les Halles on Third?

THOMAS. Yes.

MARNIE. Thor and this blonde were practically doing it right there in the restaurant.

JEFF. So that has to be the girlfriend, right? The one he strangled his wife over.

(a beat)

THOMAS. Strangled? Who said she was strangled?

JEFF. Didn't…Well, nobody. But…in most of those husband-as-the-killer cases aren't they…usually, you know, strangled?

THOMAS. I'm done here.

MARNIE. But it's possible. Suppose they were having marital problems. He learns she's having an affair. They fight. He kills her. He stashes the body in the boyfriend's home's so when the body is discovered the boyfriend looks guilty and is arrested for murder.

*(*JEFF *chokes on his drink.)*

ROBBIE. Holy Christ. That explains everything!

MARNIE. See? It's a no-brainer.

THOMAS. Especially if he's read any of your books. You are Marnie Elbies, the mystery writer?

MARNIE. Yes.

THOMAS. Doesn't that just happen to be the story-line in one of your gothic murder mysteries? What was the title… "Milady, Close Your Curtains?"

JEFF. Omigod. It is. Exactly.

ROBBIE. It is?

MIDGE. Exactly?

MARNIE. Well, yes.

(**ROBBIE** *and* **MIDGE** *are aghast.*)

MARNIE. You didn't read my book, did you? I can't believe you never read my book.

MIDGE. They all end the same.

ROBBIE. I read the dirty parts.

THOMAS. I'm leaving. I have a missing person case to solve and I've wasted enough time here with you clowns.

JEFF. But –

MARNIE. How do you explain what we saw in the window?

THOMAS. Oh, I don't know. How's about the fact that you're all drunk.

MIDGE. We weren't drinking then.

THOMAS. I don't really care. Maybe you saw Mr. Larswald drying his hair.

JEFF. What hair? Have you taken a look at that guy?

(*They all turn and look at the frightening* **THOR** *glowering at them from his apartment as he has since the beginning of this scene.*)

(*It is totally dark outside.*)

MARNIE. Does he know it's us who called?

THOMAS. Well, yeah.

MARNIE. Then we're not safe. In my book, *The Codpiece Killer*, after he murders his wife and dumps her body in a lifeboat, the –

THOMAS. Mrs. Elbies. You have to stop. We don't know that she was murdered! All we know is that she's missing and so is some of her jewelry.

(**ROBBIE** *shoots a look at* **MIDGE**.)

ROBBIE. Pearls?

THOMAS. Yes, pearls. How did you know that?

MIDGE. She always wore pearls.

    (**MARNIE, JEFF** *and* **ROBBIE** *shoot looks to* **MIDGE**.)

THOMAS. And we do know Lila had a few affairs, too, so we're –

JEFF. A few?

    (**JEFF** *looks at* **ROBBIE**. **ROBBIE** *motions "not me."*)

THOMAS. Yes. We haven't actually identified any of the men yet, but –

JEFF. None, huh?

THOMAS. Anyone here know anything about that? Seeing how you all seem to know so much.

JEFF/ROBBIE. Nope/Not me.

THOMAS. Uh huh.

JEFF. In fact, I've never been anywhere near that apartment until today.

    (**MIDGE** *looks at* **JEFF** *and gasps.* **MARNIE** *looks at* **MIDGE**.)

THOMAS. Yes?

MIDGE. Sorry. I had a dirty dog for lunch.

THOMAS. Well. That will be all for now. You leave the detective work to us.

    (*All nod and agree. In the Larswald apartment,* **THOR** *puts on a hat and jacket and exits.*)

ROBBIE. He's going out. Not that I'm looking.

THOMAS. Some words of advice. You drunks try a stunt like this again, and I'll arrest all four of you. Got me?

JEFF. Yessir.

    (*Brownout*)

    (*SFX: AC WINDS DOWN*)

MARNIE. Oh, no.

THOMAS. Dammit. I got guys in the elevators.

    (**DETECTIVE THOMAS** *exits as*)

    (*The lights come back up.*)

    (*Then the power pops back on.*)

    (*SFX: AC BLOWER STARTS UP [fade out as scene continues].*)

MIDGE. That's all we need.

    (**JEFF** *and* **ROBBIE** *exchange looks.* **MARNIE** *starts to laugh uncomfortably.*)

MARNIE. Omigod. I can't believe this.

JEFF. What?

MARNIE. I'm sorry, but you were so obvious about it, Midge.

    (*looking in the direction of* **JEFF** *and* **ROBBIE**)

Does everyone know about this but me?

MIDGE. Know what?

MARNIE. (*again in the direction of* **JEFF** *and* **ROBBIE**) About you sleeping with Lila?

    (*a beat*)

JEFF. Look, Marnie –

MARNIE. Jeff, please. Is it true? Did you, Robbie?

    (**JEFF** *reacts and takes two steps away from* **ROBBIE.**)

ROBBIE. Me? I never slept with Lila.

JEFF. Yes, you did. Yes, he did.

ROBBIE. I did not.

MIDGE. No, he didn't. But someone in this room did.

    (**MARNIE** *looks to* **MIDGE** *with a puzzled look.*)

MIDGE. Don't look at me!

    (*Everyone looks at* **JEFF.** **JEFF** *looks behind him and then back.*)

MARNIE. Jeff?

JEFF. I'm sorry, Marnie. I'm so sorry. I wanted to tell you but I didn't know how. I didn't want to hurt you.

MARNIE. Omigod.

ROBBIE. *(to* **MIDGE***)* How did you know?

MIDGE. I heard rumors in the laundry room.

(to **JEFF***)*

And then about six months ago, I saw you come out of the Larswald apartment – and just now you told the detective that you'd never been in there before today. I just put two and two together. I can't help it. I'm an accountant. I'm good with numbers. I'm sorry, Marnie.

(No one says anything. **MARNIE** *looks at* **JEFF***.)*

ROBBIE. Whew. This is awkward.

JEFF. We…we were broken up…legally.

MARNIE. I don't care!

JEFF. It was a mistake. If I could turn back the clock…

MARNIE. What, you wouldn't have me move back in? Where is she, Jeff? What's really going on? What are you two planning?

JEFF. What two? Me and Lila? Nothing is going on. It's over. Believe me.

MARNIE. I don't believe you!

ROBBIE. Oh, it's over all right.

JEFF. We were separated, remember?

MARNIE. You should have told me before I moved back. How long were you seeing her?

JEFF. It was nothing. It was a three-time fling. Four, if you count that thing in the laundry room.

MARNIE. Well, that explains why she and Thor were so weird about me moving back in. God. She's young enough to be your daughter.

JEFF. You're kidding me. I thought you two were the same age.

ROBBIE. Really?

*(***MIDGE** *smacks* **ROBBIE** *to be quiet.)*

MARNIE. Ooh. I can't even picture you kissing her. When's the last time you and she were together?

(**JEFF** *isn't sure how to answer.*)

MARNIE. Omigod. It's still going on?!

JEFF. No. Absolutely not

MARNIE. I don't believe you.

*(Behind them, we see what appears to be **LILA** cross by the window. This time "**LILA**" appears to be dragging something. The foursome does not see her.)*

JEFF. Marnie, please, I –

MARNIE. Don't come near me.

MIDGE. Come on, honey. Let's go downstairs.

ROBBIE. All right.

*(**ROBBIE** starts to follow.)*

MIDGE. Not you. Her!

JEFF. I'm sorry!

*(**MARNIE** goes to **MIDGE** and gives **JEFF** a look. The girls exit. **ROBBIE** starts to laugh.)*

What's so damm funny?

ROBBIE. You think she's mad now? Boy, when she finds out you made out with your dead girlfriend's corpse she's really gonna be pissed.

JEFF. Shut up. Do you realize how guilty I look? I had an affair with a dead girl. Her body was in my closet. I have a key to her apartment.

ROBBIE. That's how you got in there?

JEFF. Yes. Omigod. Where is the key to her apartment?

ROBBIE. Right there on the desk.

*(Behind them, "**LILA**" appears to cross the window and exit the upstage apartment. **JEFF** and **ROBBIE** don't see her.)*

JEFF. No. That's the key Marnie stole from Loomis. Where's the key that Lila gave me?…

*(It dawns on **JEFF** where the key is. He looks back at the Larswald apartment. "**LILA**" disappears from view Right before they turn. He doesn't see her. **JEFF** looks at **ROBBIE**.)*

ROBBIE. What, are you crazy? Leave it there!

JEFF. I can't! My fingerprints are all over it. Do you know how many times I used it?

ROBBIE. Three?

JEFF. I hate you.

(JEFF *picks up the key from the desk.*)

I can't believe I left it there. We've got to get that key back before anyone finds it. You sure you saw him go out?

ROBBIE. Had his hat on.

JEFF. Then let's do it now.

ROBBIE. No, we'll get caught.

JEFF. It's 39 steps away. How hard can it be?

(They exit. As they close the door to JEFF*'s apartment,* THOR *re-enters his apartment, unseen by* JEFF *and* ROBBIE*.)*

(BLACKOUT)

Scene Two

(THE LARSWALD APARTMENT – LATER)

(The Larswald apartment appears to be empty. The lights are on. It's dark outside.)

*(**THOR** enters from the kitchen with some rope and exits to the bedroom.)*

(A beat of silence.)

*(**JEFF** and **ROBBIE** slowly enter the apartment with the stolen key. **JEFF** locks the front door. They listen for a beat to make sure the coast is clear. **JEFF** motions "the kitchen." They then exit to the kitchen.)*

*(**THOR** enters from the bedroom and grabs a framed photo of **LILA** and also picks up her yoga mat. He scans the room, and exits back to the bedroom.)*

*(**JEFF** and **ROBBIE** re-enter from the kitchen – with **JEFF**'s key. He puts it in his right pocket and wipes his brow. "That was a close one.")*

*(**JEFF** and **ROBBIE** sneak to the front door. As they reach for the door handle someone tries to open it from the other side.)*

*(They panic, back up, and go to hide in the closet. As **JEFF** opens the closet, the lifeless body of **LILA LARSWALD** is revealed, hanging on the back of the closet door. **JEFF** and **ROBBIE**, who have not seen the body, jump into the closet and pull the door closed behind them by yanking on the dead girl's arm.)*

(a beat)

*(The front door opens. **MIDGE** tiptoes into the apartment, dressed in a black T-shirt and black jeans. She carries a large strand of pearls.)*

*(She hears a noise at the closet door and hides behind the sofa. **JEFF** peeks out of the closet, sees the coast is clear. **JEFF** and **ROBBIE** leap out of the closet, closing the door behind them. They have silent fits at being in the closet with the corpse. **ROBBIE** breathes deeply.)*

MIDGE. Robbie?

(JEFF *and* ROBBIE *turn, see* MIDGE *and yelp.*)

JEFF. Midge?

MIDGE. Jesus Christ, you almost gave me a heart attack.

ROBBIE. Yeah? Well, go in the closet. That'll finish you off.

JEFF. How the hell did you get in here?

MIDGE. The door was open.

JEFF. No, it wasn't.

MIDGE. Was so.

JEFF. You're a liar!

ROBBIE. Midge! You promised.

JEFF. That door was locked.

MIDGE. Okay. I used a credit card. Happy? What are you two doing in here?

JEFF. Why are you dressed like that? And what's with the pearls?

MIDGE. All right. I confess. I stole them.

JEFF. What?

MIDGE. I have a little problem, okay? I'm putting them back before I'm blamed for something I didn't do.

ROBBIE. I thought your therapist said you were over that.

JEFF. Over…You're a cat burglar?

ROBBIE. No, just jewelry.

MIDGE. Hey, at least I don't cheat on my wife.

ROBBIE. They were legally separated.

MIDGE. Yeah, but you weren't. Why do you have naked pictures of Lila in your secret underwear drawer, Robbie?

ROBBIE. I was holding them for Jeff.

MIDGE. Get away from me. You're both pigs.

JEFF. I don't understand any of this.

(re: closet)

Where did Lila come from?

MIDGE. Ireland, why?

JEFF. No, I –

(They hear **THOR** *coughing in the bedroom.)*

ROBBIE. Omigod. Thor's still in here. He's coming!

JEFF. The closet. Quick.

*(***ROBBIE** *runs for the closet door and opens it.* **JEFF** *grabs* **MIDGE** *and pulls her into the closet. The dead body swings closed on them again.)*

MIDGE. Is that – ?

*(***MIDGE** *starts to scream. The men quickly muffle her.)*

(Upstage, we see **MARNIE** *in her apartment looking through the window.)*

*(***THOR** *enters from his bedroom, pushing a steamer trunk on a dolly. A pink terry cloth bathrobe hangs out.)*

THOR. The rope.

(He leaves the steamer trunk on the dolly and starts to exit back into the bedroom.)

*(***THOR** *sees the pearls on the sofa, picks them up, questions why they're there, and exits to the bedroom with them, muttering to himself.)*

(The threesome peeks out of the closet. **JEFF** *keeps his hand on* **MIDGE***'s mouth.)*

ROBBIE. The coast is clear.

JEFF. Did he leave?

ROBBIE. I think so.

MIDGE. *(pulling his hand away)* Omigod! She's dead! She's dead!

*(***JEFF** *muffles her.)*

JEFF. We know that. Shut up!

ROBBIE. Who hung her in the closet?

JEFF. Wasn't me. I laid her in the tub.

MIDGE. *(pulling his hand away)* You did what to her in the tub?

*(***JEFF** *puts his hand over her mouth.)*

JEFF. Shut up. The cops said they searched the place. What's Lila's body doing hanging in the closet?

(*JEFF sees the steamer trunk.*)

What the hell is that?

(**ROBBIE** *sees the terry cloth robe hanging out of the trunk.*)

ROBBIE. Oh, Jesus. The robe. Look at the robe. The girl who walked past the window. She's in the trunk!

JEFF. Who is she?

ROBBIE. I don't know.

(*They step towards the trunk. They exchange looks. They don't see* **MARNIE** *waving and warning them that* **THOR** *is in the bedroom. Behind them,* **MARNIE** *runs out the door of her apartment.*)

JEFF. Let's open it and find out.

(**MIDGE** *struggles to get away.* **JEFF** *holds her firm.*)

(**THOR** *makes noise in the bedroom.*)

ROBBIE. Wait. Ssh.

(*listens and points off to the bedroom*)

Oh, shit. It's Thor!

JEFF. You said he left!

(**JEFF** *and* **ROBBIE** *run in opposite directions, pulling* **MIDGE** *apart between them.* **JEFF** *lets go.* **ROBBIE** *drags* **MIDGE** *back into the closet.* **JEFF** *quickly ducks behind the trunk as* **THOR** *re-enters from the bedroom with the rope.*)

(**THOR** *ties the trunk with the rope.*)

THOR. I should've done this years ago. Goddamn tramp.

(**THOR** *pushes the dolly with the trunk out the front door.* **JEFF** *dives behind the couch as* **THOR** *passes by.* **THOR** *exits, leaving the front door ajar. Silence.*)

(*Suddenly there is a Brownout.*)

(*Then a BLACKOUT.*)

(SFX: AC POWERS DOWN.)

(In the moonlight, we see forms but nothing clear enough to distinguish who's who or what's what.)

(In the dark we hear:)

(SFX: LOUD OFFSTAGE CRASH stage right and a PAINFUL SCREAM)

(silence)

(SFX: THE POWER COMES BACK ON.)

(SFX: AC BLOWER STARTS UP [fade out as scene continues].)

(Lights up full.)

(The apartment appears to be empty.)

*(The closet door slowly opens. **MIDGE** and **ROBBIE** tiptoe out, leaving **LILA** hanging on the open door. **MARNIE** and **JEFF** pop up from behind the sofa. They all jump. **MIDGE** is losing it. **JEFF** covers her mouth.)*

MARNIE. You have to get out of here.

ROBBIE. No shit, Sherlock. He took the trunk with the dead girl in it.

MARNIE. What?

MIDGE. Don't kill me. Don't kill me.

JEFF. Shut up. I know where your earrings are, Marnie!

*(**MIDGE** is incoherent and begging. **JEFF** shoves his hand over her mouth.)*

MARNIE. You're a cat burglar?

JEFF/ROBBIE. No. Just jewelry!

JEFF. Ew. Stop licking me.

MARNIE. What's that smell?

*(**ROBBIE** opens the closet door.)*

JEFF. Thor strangled his wife and hung her in the closet.

*(**MARNIE** turns and sees **LILA**'s lifeless body swinging on the door. She screams at the top of her lungs.)*

ROBBIE. I hope nobody heard that.

JEFF. Let's get out of here.

*(Suddenly a frightening and bloody **THOR** appears from the kitchen dragging his foot. He lets out a horrible, anguished howl. They all scream, as once again the city BLACKS OUT.)*

(Faint moonlight lights up the courtyard outside the window. We cannot see who's who or what's what.)

(In the dark we hear:)

ALL. Help! Help!/Somebody help us!/Police! Call the police!/Murder! Fire!

JEFF. Come on! Move, move, move!

*(We immediately hear them all running. The door to **THOR**'s apartment opens and closes as they flee.)*

(COMPLETE BLACKOUT)

Scene Three

(APARTMENT HALLWAY – CONTINUOUS)

(The following is all heard in the pitch black [played downstage as the set is changed behind them].)

JEFF. Give me your hand. It's pitch black in this hallway.

MARNIE. Somebody help!!!

(SFX: FIRE TRUCKS)

(Street noises drown out their calls for help, as **MARNIE** *pounds on a door in the dark.)*

ROBBIE. No sense yelling. Nellie's in the Hamptons and the other apartment's being painted. We're all alone on this floor!

JEFF. Keep moving.

MIDGE. Where are we? Is this a door knob? It's all wet.

JEFF. Please stop turning that. That's me.

MARNIE. Wait a minute. Where's Thor?

JEFF. I don't know.

(silence)

(SFX: NYC TRAFFIC)

MARNIE. What happened to Lila, Jeff?

JEFF. Thor killed Lila and stuffed her in our closet to try and frame me. But we found the body first and put it back in his apartment.

MARNIE. You did what?

ROBBIE. But the cops couldn't find her, so we went back in there and found her dead again. She is dead.

MIDGE. She's dead, Marnie. She's so dead.

MARNIE. Omigod. I knew it.

ROBBIE. And there's somebody else dead in a trunk wearing a terry cloth bathrobe.

MARNIE. What?

JEFF. Where's a phone? We need a phone.

THOR. *(off)* Where are you? I'll kill all of you! I'll see you in hell!

MARNIE. Omigod. Jeff, in case something happens...I forgive you for Lila.

JEFF. Why? Because she's dead?

MARNIE. No. When we were separated and I was in L.A...I had an affair with my editor Ian.

JEFF. The guy with the six-pack abs? That's what you want me to think about as I meet my Maker?

MARNIE. I didn't want you to die feeling guilty.

JEFF. Great. Now I'm gonna die sick to my stomach.

MARNIE. I didn't want that on my chest.

ROBBIE. He was on your chest?

VOICE. What is wrong with you people?

(silence)

JEFF. Who the hell is that?

LOOMIS. It's me, Loomis. What's going on?

JEFF. Thor Larswald killed his wife. Now he's after us.

LOOMIS. Christ, it's always something in this building.

MIDGE. Loomis. Get help!

LOOMIS. Help? I'm getting the hell out of here. Hey. What are you doing here? No, no. Don't.

(SFX: FOOTSTEPS, RUNNING, AND A LOUD THUMP)

*(**LOOMIS** groans.)*

MIDGE. Loomis?

JEFF. He's down! Run!

*(**JEFF**, **MARNIE MIDGE** and **ROBBIE** run for their lives.)*

(BLACKOUT)

Scene Four

(JEFF & MARNIE'S APARTMENT – CONTINUOUS)

(Moonlight spills in the courtyard window.)

(Although movement is given in stage directions, we can't really tell who's who or what's what.)

(The door opens, four bodies rush inside.)

JEFF. Quick, get in. It's our apartment. Move!

(The front door closes.)

MARNIE. I'll get some flashlights.

*(**MARNIE** moves off to the kitchen.)*

ROBBIE. I'll find the phone.

*(**ROBBIE** crosses in and smacks into the coffee table.)*

(SFX: ROBBIE WALKS INTO A TABLE)

Your mother's ass.

JEFF. Marnie, hurry.

(SFX: NOISE FROM RUMMAGING IN DRAWERS)

*(**MARNIE** enters from the kitchen with four flashlights.)*

MARNIE. I'm here. Here, Jeff. And next time, put the pie back in the refrigerator when you're done. Here. Midge. Robbie.

ROBBIE. Right here.

(silence)

(One by one flashlights go on. We see nothing but the lights. The flashlights blind the audience for a few beats.)

JEFF. Marnie?

MARNIE. Right here.

(She moves her flashlight up and down so we know it's her.)

MARNIE. Jeff?

JEFF. Right here.

(He moves his flashlight up and down so we know it's him.)

JEFF. Robbie?

ROBBIE. Over here.

(He moves his flashlight up and down so we know it's him.)

Midge? Is that you?

(A fourth flashlight moves up and down.)

Midge?

*(**ROBBIE** shines the light on his own face so everyone can see it's him.)*

*(**MARNIE** shines the light on her own face so everyone can see it's her.)*

*(**JEFF** shines the light on his own face so everyone can see it's him.)*

*(**THOR** shines the fourth light on himself.)*

(Everyone screams. The flashlights are clicked off.)

(After a beat of silence we see the light of two flashlights enter from stage right. One circles around the back of the sofa. One walks directly to center. The two lights meet at center, bang into each other, and fall to the floor. The light right centerstage slowly rises. A third light enters from the archway stage right headed for center. The right stage center flashlight sees this and tries to flee stage left tripping over the left stage center flashlight who is still on the ground. He falls. The stage right flashlight trips on the two centerstage flashlights, and falls to the ground.)

(From stage right the fourth flashlight enters, runs around the back of the sofa and exits stage left.)

*(The other three flash their lights on each other — **MARNIE**, **JEFF**, and **ROBBIE**. **MIDGE** is there, too. They shine light on each other and scream.)*

JEFF. Thor's still in here. Let's get out of here.

MARNIE. Maybe the elevator's working.

(They run out the stage left door, unaware they are following the fourth flashlight.)

(A beat of silence. A scream. One by one, three flashlights return in a run.)

ROBBIE. How does that guy always know where we are?

MARNIE. I don't know!

JEFF. Marnie?

MARNIE. I'm here.

JEFF. Robbie?

ROBBIE. Yo. Midge?

MIDGE. Back here.

JEFF. Then the next one in is him! Turn your lights out. Here he comes. One, two, three!

(A fourth flashlight enters. He is knocked unconscious by a series of blows from **JEFF** *and* **MARNIE***'s flashlights.)*

(SFX: FLASHLIGHT REPEATEDLY HITTING SKULL)

We got him!

(SFX: POWER BACK ON)

(Lights up full.)

(Suddenly the power comes back on and the lights come up. The front door is wide open. A man lies on the floor. It's not **THOR***.)*

MIDGE. Thank God. Call the cops.

*(***ROBBIE** *runs for the phone. He hits the coffee table again.)*

ROBBIE. Your father's balls.

MARNIE. Oh, no. Oh, no! Jeff! It's the wrong man. It's not Thor Larswald. We knocked out Detective Thomas!

*(***MARNIE** *kneels down to help* **DETECTIVE THOMAS***.)*

JEFF. That means Thor is still in here somewhere.

(They all look slowly at each other and around the room.)

(The lights black out again.)

ROBBIE. Shitaki mushrooms.

MIDGE. Is it every building? Or just ours?

MARNIE. Where is he, Jeff?

JEFF. I don't know.

(*Fireworks explode lighting up the courtyard and apartment intermittently throughout the following.*)

(*Everyone jumps.*)

Thank God for the Fourth of July. Some light.

MIDGE. They're so loud! We're all gonna die and no one will hear us scream.

ROBBIE. (*at phone*) I still can't get through.

JEFF. Marnie. Get the detective's gun.

(**MARNIE** *searches for* **THOMAS**' *gun.*)

MARNIE. It's gone.

(*They look around, unsure of what to do.*)

(*SFX: DRAWER OF SILVERWARE FALLS TO THE GROUND IN THE KITCHEN*)

ROBBIE. What's that?

(**JEFF** *motions "stand back," takes his flashlight and starts toward the kitchen.*)

(*Another explosion of fireworks.*)

(*Lit up in the red lights of the fireworks and* **JEFF**'s *flashlight,* **THOR LARSWALD** *appears in the kitchen archway. He moves slow and scary. Everyone jumps back.*)

(**THOR** *arches up, grabbing at his back. He turns revealing scissors protruding from between his shoulder blades. He grabs at them, but can't reach them. He collapses onto the floor.* **MARNIE** *screams at the top of her lungs.*)

JEFF. You've gotta stop doing that.

(**THOR** *twitches a little, then stops.*)

MIDGE. Omigod.

(**JEFF** *goes into the kitchen.*)

MARNIE. Jeff, no!

(The lights come back on.)

ROBBIE. Who stabbed him!? Who did that!?

*(A beat. **JEFF** returns.)*

JEFF. There's nobody in there. Whoever did that to him must have run past us in the dark. Unless it was one of us.

(Everyone looks at each other suspiciously.)

MARNIE. Is he alive?

*(**JEFF** tentatively takes **THOR**'s pulse. He shakes his head.)*

JEFF. No. He's...he's dead.

THOR. You...

(They all jump.)

JEFF. I stand corrected.

THOR. You stole...Lila....took her from me.

JEFF. Yeah, but...then I gave her back...

THOR. You didn't have to kill her!

(coughing fit)

Why'd you have to kill her?

*(**THOR** has a coughing fit and then stops moving.)*

MARNIE. Oh, God.

MIDGE. Is he...?

JEFF. I don't know. I'm not checking him again.

*(**JEFF** looks up to see everyone looking at him.)*

ROBBIE. He said YOU killed Lila.

JEFF. Oh, come on. I didn't kill her. He killed her.

*(to **THOR**)*

Right, Thor? Didn't you, Thor? Tell them, Thor. Oh, Thor.

MARNIE. He said you killed her. Why does he think you killed her, Jeff?

JEFF. I don't know. He's a liar. It had to be him. Look, he knew about Lila and me. He sent me naked photos of Lila and stuffed her body in our closet to incriminate me. Who else could it be?

MARNIE. I don't know.

JEFF. Why on earth would I want to kill Lila?

ROBBIE. Well, maybe because Marnie was moving back home and Lila threatened to expose your affair. So you had to kill her. And you used those photos to make me think you were being blackmailed by Thor, when in fact, they were your photos to begin with.

(*The others all look at* JEFF.)

JEFF. That's ridiculous. It's just as plausible that Marnie found out about Lila and me and killed her in a jealous rage and then framed me for the murder just like in her book.

(*Everyone looks at* MARNIE.)

MARNIE. Oh, please. Midge could have killed Lila when she stole her jewelry and then used your affair as a cover to fake her own innocence.

(*Everyone looks at* MIDGE.)

MIDGE. Oh, come on. You don't believe that. You might as well say that Robbie had an affair with Lila and killed her when she threatened to tell everyone he can't stop laughing after he ejaculates.

(*Everyone looks at* ROBBIE.)

ROBBIE. Well, that was unnecessary.

(*No one moves. No one trusts anyone else. They all stare at each other.*)

MARNIE. So…now what?

JEFF. I'm telling you, it's Thor. How else do you explain the dead body in the trunk. The girlfriend in the restaurant. Why he was covered in blood.

(THOR *stirs.*)

THOR. Trunk...

(All jump.)

JEFF. Jesus Christ. He's like a cockroach.

THOR. ...trunk filled with Lila's...clothes....throwing them ...in incinerator. BLACKOUT... fell down...stairs...

(Another fireworks explosion.)

MARNIE. What about the blonde you were hugging at Les Halles?

THOR. ...My...sister Rebecca.

ROBBIE. But you tried to kill us!

THOR. Saw...Lila...

(coughs heavily)

...thought you killed her.

MARNIE. Omigod, he's innocent!

ROBBIE. Shouldn't we get this guy a doctor or something?

MARNIE. You poor man.

JEFF. Wait a minute. If Thor didn't kill Lila...who did?

(Another fireworks explosion.)

(SFX: THEME TO "PSYCHO"-SOUNDING CLOSET DOOR SQUEAK)

*(**LOOMIS** enters from the closet in a long, curly brown wig and pink terry cloth robe with a knife. Everyone screams. He stabs the air, bathed in the eerie light of the fireworks. All back away. **LOOMIS** corrals them with the knife.)*

Loomis?

LOOMIS. Yeah, Loomis.

MARNIE. You killed Lila?

LOOMIS. I told you I did. It's always the handyman, remember? Slut deserved it. She slept with everyone in this building. She was notorious.

*(re: **ROBBIE**)*

She even did laughing boy over there.

*(**THOR** moans. **ROBBIE** motions "not me.")*

LOOMIS. *(cont.)* But not old Loomis! Oh, yes, she'd tease me with her tight little body, asking for it, but when I finally came on to her she laughed at me. Right in my face. So I went into this frenzy and choked the smirk right off her slutty little puss. Oh, sure. She'd sleep with a psycho who's so afraid of birds he can't leave the building. She'd sleep with that shitting asshole Mr. MacGuffin. But not me!

(makes game show buzzer noise)

Not Loomis!

JEFF. Why did you put her in our closet?

LOOMIS. So they'd blame you. Who better than the lover that dumped her because his wife was coming back. This way they'd find her in your apartment along with those naked photos. And nobody'd suspect me. It's a great plan.

MARNIE. I know. It's from one of my books.

LOOMIS. Where do you think I got it from? Told you I'm a big fan, Mrs. Elbies. And it would have worked perfectly but Birdman here had to move the body to the Larswalds' tub and screw everything up. I knew you would call the cops, so I walked past the window pretending to be Lila to throw you off.

ROBBIE. *(staring at* **LOOMIS** *in a wig and terry robe)* Holy shit, that was you?

LOOMIS. But I was too late. The cops were on their way. So I stashed her in the apartment I was painting and moved her back when they left. Luckily, the paint fumes covered the stink. She's in your tub right now. And they're gonna arrest you for the whole thing.

JEFF. What are you talking about? There are four of us here that know the truth.

THOR. *(in a weak voice)* Five.

(All jump.)

MARNIE. You'll never get away with this.

LOOMIS. *(makes game show buzzer noise)* Oh, but I will get away with it. I'm going to kill all of you and frame Mr. Elbies. Larwald's already coughing up blood bubbles, so only four more to go.

(**ROBBIE** *quickly grabs the knife out of* **LOOMIS**' *hand.*)

ROBBIE. Yeah? Well, whose got the upper hand now, you low-life piece of shit?

(**LOOMIS** *pulls out the detective's gun.*)

LOOMIS. I believe it's still me.

(**LOOMIS** *points gun at* **ROBBIE**.)

Drop it.

(**ROBBIE** *does.* **LOOMIS** *kicks it away. The knife slides across the room. It pierces* **THOR** *between the legs. His butt pops up in the air and falls back down.*)

THOR. Ow.

(**THOR** *pounds the ground in agony.*)

LOOMIS. Okay, Mr. Elbies. Now, get out on that ledge or I'll shoot your wife in the face.

JEFF. Oh, come on, now.

(*He points the gun in* **MARNIE**'s *face.*)

JEFF. Wait, wait, wait. Look, if you throw me off the ledge the cops'll know I was pushed.

(**LOOMIS** *opens the window.*)

LOOMIS. I won't have to throw you anywhere. You're going to jump all on your own with no help from me. And everyone will think you killed yourself after slaughtering everyone else. And then you can all be buried together in a nice little family plot.

(**LOOMIS** *puts the gun to* **MARNIE**'s *head.*)

Now get out there.

JEFF. I'm going. I'm going. I love you, Marnie. I'll always love you.

MARNIE. I love you, too.

LOOMIS. Get out there.

(**JEFF** *starts to go out, hesitates, and then steps out onto the ledge.*)

(*Another fireworks explosion.*)

Like the fireworks? Like how they're lighting up the sky? Makes it look like daylight, don't it? And guess what comes out in the daylight?

(*SFX: PIGEONS COOING*)

Birds!!!

(**JEFF** *freaks out and hyperventilates.*)

MARNIE. Jeff. God, don't do this, Loomis.

(**JEFF** *wavers. A bird flies at him. He swats at it, teeters, loses his balance and falls off the ledge, screaming as he goes.* **MARNIE** *screams.* **MIDGE** *passes out.* **ROBBIE** *goes to her.*)

MARNIE. Omigod, no! Jeff!!!!

(**MARNIE** *attacks* **LOOMIS**. *She jumps on him and starts beating the sides of his face with her fists.*)

LOOMIS. Ahhh!

(*He tries to swat her off. The gun goes flying.* **MARNIE** *leaps off* **LOOMIS** *and jumps on the gun.* **LOOMIS** *jumps on* **MARNIE**. **ROBBIE** *leaves* **MIDGE**, *and jumps on* **LOOMIS**. *The pile-up rolls across the floor. They point the gun away from their bodies. To the left. To the right. To the left.*)

(*SFX: GUNSHOT*)

THOR. Ah, Jesus.

(**THOR** *grabs his ass.*)

(*The tussle between* **LOOMIS**, **MARNIE** *and* **ROBBIE** *continues.*)

(*The pile-up rolls across the floor, the opposite direction. They point the gun away from their bodies. To the left. To the right. To the left.*)

(SFX: GUNSHOT)

THOR. *(cont.)* Ah, for Christ's Sake.

(The gun disappears inside the pile-up.)

(SFX: GUNSHOT)

(A beat of silence.)

(ROBBIE *rolls off, shot in the shoulder as the gun skids across the floor. He lies there in agony, unable to move.)*

(Behind them, **JEFF** *climbs back up onto the ledge. He is covered in live birds and droppings as other birds fly at his head. He bravely crosses the ledge to the open window, batting, punching and tossing the birds aside one by one.)*

(DETECTIVE THOMAS *comes to. Disoriented. But aware enough to see as* **LOOMIS** *starts to choke* **MARNIE.** **MARNIE** *fights back but is losing.)*

LOOMIS. I'll kill you, too. Just like I killed that bitch Lila.

(MARNIE *makes gurgling noises as she is choked.)*

What? Sorry, I can't understand you. What are you saying? Squeeze tighter? Oh, okay.

(He chokes the life out of **MARNIE.** *Out on the ledge,* **JEFF** *knocks the birds off his shoulders.* **JEFF** *leaps into the apartment, disheveled with feathers in his hair.)*

JEFF. Get the hell off of her!

(JEFF *pulls* **LOOMIS** *off* **MARNIE** *by grabbing his head and smashing his face into the floor five times.* **JEFF** *tosses* **LOOMIS** *aside like a rag doll.)*

You know how much I tipped you last Christmas!?

(JEFF *goes to* **MARNIE** *pulling her to him in a desperate embrace.* **DETECTIVE THOMAS** *locates his gun.)*

Are you all right?

MARNIE. I thought you were dead.

JEFF. Thank God for Mr. McGuffin's pigeon coop. Those birds saved my life.

(They kiss. When they break, they cough. A few bird feathers fly out of their mouths.)

*(**DETECTIVE THOMAS** keeps his gun trained on **LOOMIS** as he dials his cell phone.)*

THOMAS. *(into phone)* Jesus, I got a mess up here. Four-oh-six. I repeat, four-oh-six. Need immediate EMS, 140 East 28th Street, apartment 10B. I got three down. Gun shot victim. Fatal stabbing –

THOR. *(in a weak voice)* I'm still alive.

THOMAS. Jesus Christ. He's still alive. Step on it, Harry. From where you are, take Third. Right. North by northwest. Right.

*(**DETECTIVE THOMAS** closes his cell phone. **MIDGE** starts to wake up.)*

*(to **THOR**)* Don't move, sir. Help's on the way. And as for you, shitbird…

*(**THOMAS** cuffs the still unconscious **LOOMIS**.)*

*(**MIDGE** crawls to **ROBBIE** and cradles his head.)*

MIDGE. Robbie. Omigod! Are you okay?

ROBBIE. Yeah, but these pants are ruined!

THOMAS. Why are you dressed like that? What are you, a cat burglar?

JEFF/MARNIE/ROBBIE/MIDGE. No, just jewelry.

MIDGE. Oh, Robbie. After we get you fixed up, what say we go downstairs and have a few laughs?

ROBBIE. As long as you promise I get the last laugh…

MIDGE. Don't you always?

(They kiss.)

MARNIE. Oh, Jeff. You weren't even afraid. I can't believe how brave you were.

JEFF. Ah, they were just birds. Stinking, lice-ridden, eye-pecking birds. I'm just so glad I didn't lose you.

MARNIE. You're never going to lose me. And I'm never going to leave you again.

THOR. For Christ's sake, could I have some water?

THOMAS. Jeez, you're still with us?

(into cell)

Where the hell are you guys? Yeah? Well, then you drive. The trouble with Harry is…

(DETECTIVE THOMAS *runs off to the kitchen.)*

MARNIE. Oh, this is all going to make one helluva bestseller. And I'm going to name the hero "Jeff." After you. You knew just what to do. All along you knew so much. You knew more than enough.

JEFF. What are you going to call the book? "The Man Who Knew Too Much?"

(He chuckles.)

MARNIE. "Manhattan Murder Mystery."

(They kiss. Behind them fierworks light up the sky.)

(CURTAIN)

PROPERTY LIST

Badge (Police Detective)
Bath Towel
Batteries for Flashlights
Binoculars (Large)
Binoculars (Small)
Blonde Wig
Brown Lunch Bag
Brown Wig
Bundle of Mail in Rubber Band
Cardboard Periscope
Cell Phone
Champagne Bottle (Unopened)
Champagne Bottle (Open, filled with ginger ale)
Champagne Glasses (4 + spares)
Cleaning Supplies
Crashpad (outside ledge)
Credit Card (NY Mets Visa)
Crow
Feathers (loose)
Flashlights (4, working)
Flyers ("Missing")
Flying Pigeon
Framed Photo of Lila
Ginger Ale
Gun (shoots)
Hand Cart
Handcuffs
Janitor's Master Key Ring
Keys (40 Identical)
Knife (Large)
Manilla Envelope
Martini Glasses (4 + spares)
Newspaper (rolled and bagged in plastic)
Pearl Necklace
Pencil
Pigeon(s)
Polaroids of Marisa Naked
Police Holster
Porno Magazines (Small stack)
Prop Blood
Purses (2)
Rope (White)
Rubber Gloves
Scissors

Scissors in Back Gag (to match scissors in earlier scene)
Seagull(s)
Steamer Trunk
Suitcase (Smallish)
Terry Bathrobe (Plus scrap to hang from steamer trunk)
Tool Box (2) with tools ("Electric box" and "Fix-it box")
Toothbrush
Towel
Yoga Mat

COSTUME PLOT

A1:Sc1   Early evening, summer, NYC

MARNIE ELBIES: summer cocktail dress, hi-heels

JEFF ELBIES: summer-weight suit, shirt and tie

ROBBIE: summer-weight suit, shirt and tie

MIDGE: summer cocktail dress, hi-heels

THOR LARSWALD: white "wife beater" undershirt, khaki slacks (work pants), work boots

LILA LARSWALD: form fitting yoga ensemble: Capri leggings, sleeveless cropped crossover top

A1:Sc2, 3 Two days later, afternoon

MARNIE ELBIES: pencil skirt, summer blouse, heels, handbag

JEFF ELBIES: slim cut, summer cotton trousers, short sleeve button down shirt. Add baseball hat for Sc:3

MIDGE: cotton Capri pants, summer blouse w/ button front, flats, hand bag/tote bag

LOOMIS: dark work pants, light grey or striped short sleeve uniform shirt (both w/ paint spatters), tool belt, large key ring detachable from belt, work boots

ROBBIE: summer cotton trousers, polo shirt

THOR LARSWALD: add work shirt to A:1

A1:Sc4   Next morning

MARNIE ELBIES: Oversize man's (JEFF's) dress shirt. Then, cotton slim cut pants, summer blouse, wedge sandals

JEFF ELBIES: summer cotton trousers, short sleeve button down or polo shirt

ROBBIE: summer cotton trousers, polo shirt

MIDGE: summer pants or capris, summer blouse, flats, hand bag

LOOMIS: same

LILA LARSWALD: Capri pants, sexy blouse over harness

LILA double: heavy terrycloth bathrobe, towel

A2:Sc1   That evening
MARNIE: same as 1:4
JEFF: same as 1:4
MIDGE: same as 1:4
ROBBIE: same as 1:4
DETECTIVE DOYLE THOMAS: unremarkable single breasted suit, white shirt, tie, shoulder harness
TWO NYC PATROLMEN: midnight blue short sleeve police uniforms

A2:Sc2, 3 Later that evening
MARNIE: same as 1: 4
JEFF: same as 1:4
ROBBIE: same as 1:4
MIDGE: black jeans, long sleeve black t-shirt or turtleneck, black flats or Keds
THOR: same as 1:1
LILA: same as 1:4
LOOMIS: same
DETECTIVE THOMAS: same

Colors: light- pastels or bights and neutrals (khaki, grey) solids for all but MIDGE

Fabrics: summer weight woven cotton or cotton/lycra blends for most

Silhouettes should be slim, stylish w/ early 60'sfeel

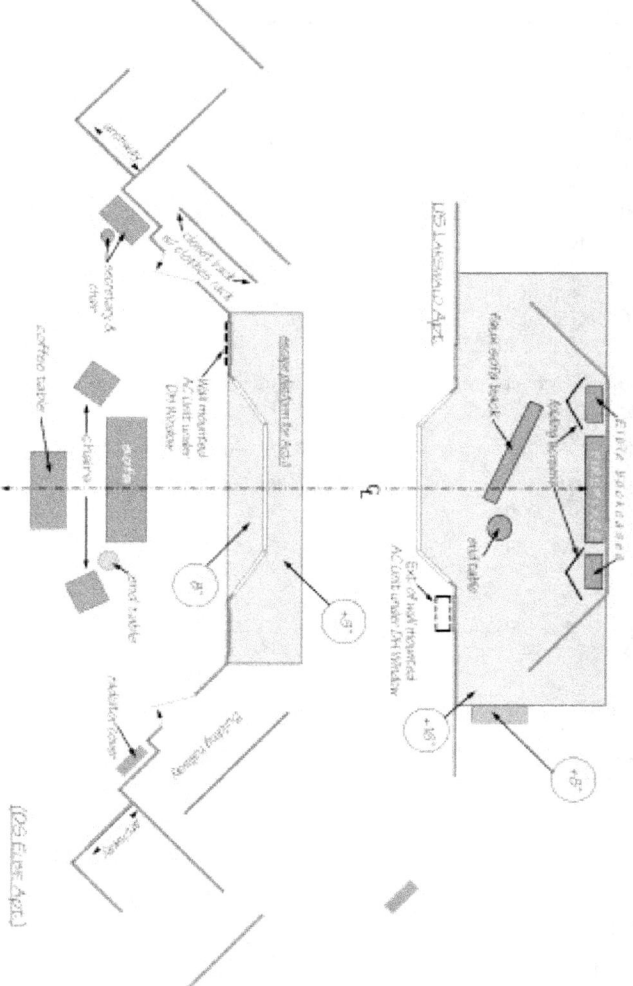

"Wrong Window" Set Floor Plan

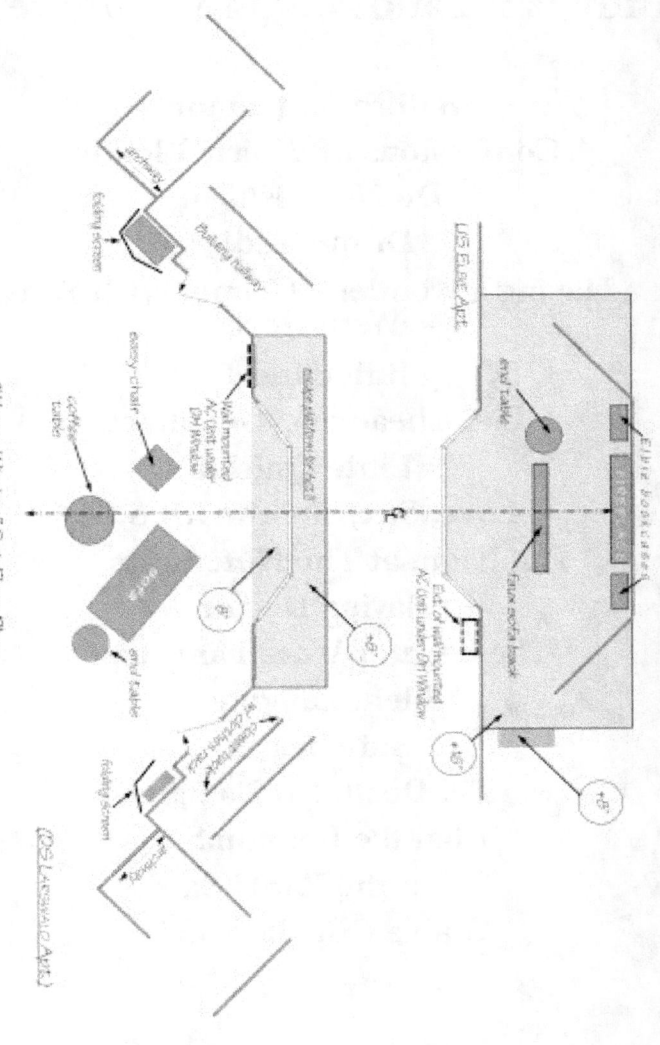

"Wrong Window" Set Floor Plan

(DS Landwood Apt.)

US Elise Apt.

Also by
Billy Van Zandt & Jane Milmore...

Bathroom Humor

Confessions of a Dirty Blonde

Do Not Disturb

Drop Dead!

Having a Wonderful Time, Wish You Were Her!

Infidelities!

Lie, Cheat, and Genuflect

A Little Quickie

Love, Sex, and the I.R.S.

A Night at The Nutcracker

Playing Doctor

The Senator Wore Pantyhose

Silent Laughter

Suitehearts

Till Death Do Us Part

What the Bellhop Saw

What the Rabbi Saw

You've Got Hate Mail

Please visit our website **samuelfrench.com** for complete descriptions and licensing information.